THE ASSASSIN HEIRESS

CORINNE M. KNIGHT

GUANYIN
PUBLISHING

Copyright notice

Written and published by Corinne M. Knight

Edited by Karen Sanders Editing

Alpha Read by Alpha Reading by TS Arthur

Cover by Covers by Jo

To my procrastination, for always keeping me company during my writing process. You've taught me the art of finding inspiration in the most unexpected places, like the bottom of a snack bag or the depths of TikTok. This book wouldn't have been the same without your timely distractions.

"..the world seems full of good men--even if there are monsters in it."

Bram Stoker, Dracula

BLURB

Alessandra de Winter has always known nothing but the life of an academy student and an assassin.

When she gains new supernatural powers, she makes the bold decision to set aside her dark legacy and embark on a quest to find her missing father. Convinced that his extraordinary abilities hold the key to defeating the enigmatic leader of the Order, Alessandra vanishes into the night with her companions, Jade and Ash, leaving behind her lover Vlad Dracula and the familiar halls of the academy she once called home.

But as Alessandra treads on a dangerous path, will her secret alliance with the Prince of Hell and an overpowered witch prove to be the solution to all her gripping challenges? Or will she be ensnared in a web of darkness that leads to her ultimate downfall?

Meanwhile, Vlad learns of the trio's capture by the Order and takes matters into his own hands, embarking on a heart-pounding journey to the stronghold of the organisation. Will his daring choice be the turning point in the supernatural war, or has he unwittingly delivered the very means the Order needs to annihilate their enemies and claim victory?

Chapter 1

Roslyn Academy

Alessandra squinted against the darkness, her eyes slowly adjusting to the faint reddish glow glinting off the walls. Shards of glass crunched beneath her feet as she took a tentative step forward. She saw Avery in the corner, tucked into a foetal position on the hard iron bed, motionless and unaware of their presence.

She looked up at Jade with wide eyes, her heart pounding in her chest. "Did you send us back in time?"

Jade shook her head. "No. I tapped into the magic lingering from Avery's last few moments here. We'll need to act quickly before they fade."

Vlad voiced his curiosity from behind them. "What's the plan?"

"I didn't have one," Jade said, her hands shaking and her eyes blazing with determination. "I saw an opportunity and seized it. With any luck, this will give us some answers about who kidnapped her."

Jade was trembling, but she stood firm beside Ash as the two huge demons appeared in the cell. They had an ominous air about them that seemed to fill the room like a physical weight, and Ash let out a furious roar. "Amon and Shax! How dare you enter here!" But the monsters ignored him, their attention fixed on Avery.

Jade's voice wavered but remained steady as she whispered, "They can't hear you, my love."

The demons eyed Avery menacingly, their

yellow eyes glinting in the dim light. One of them stepped forward and snarled, "Your father sent us to take you back home, sweetheart. If you don't cooperate, the only thing he will get is your rotting corpse."

Avery's lips twitched into a bitter smile as she replied, her voice dripping with venomous rage. "Ah, so the old man is calling his creation home? Let's see how he likes it when I'm done with him." The other demon let out a guttural chuckle and produced a leather sack filled with dark powder. With precise movements, they began tracing symbols onto the walls and floor. Avery watched with curiosity as the patterns revealed themselves in black dust.

Avery shifted her gaze from the golden box to Jade and then away again, her eyes glassy with resignation. Her mouth opened, though no sound emerged. Finally, her quiet words were emitted with a hint of desperation. "Do not look for me."

The demons encircled Avery, their malevolent grins widening as they chanted in a demonic tongue that reverberated off the walls. She thrashed against their iron grip and screamed until her voice went hoarse, but it was futile. In the blink of an eye, they vanished in a puff of sulfuric smoke that floated up to the ceiling, leaving only the scent of brimstone behind.

Alessandra's eyes were ablaze with fury as she glared at Ash. She was shaking, her heart pounding as if it would break out of her chest. Her voice quivered when she spoke. "Tell me everything you know before I send you to the abyss to join them!"

Jade stepped in between them, one hand raised like a shield. Her voice was cautious but firm. "Alessandra, be careful. He may know who they are, but that doesn't mean he's responsible for what happened."

Alessandra allowed herself one fleeting glance at Lucien, who was supported by Vlad on one side, his whole body trembling and his shoulders slumped. Despite her anger, her heart broke for him. Lucien loved Avery with all his being. Seeing her being taken must have been devastating for him too.

Ash snarled back at her, "Those guys are Marquis of Hell. Mercenaries and nothing more, but they're ruthless. Wait until I get my hands on them."

Lucien shifted his weight, bringing attention to himself. "They mentioned Avery's father. Do you think he could be behind all this demonic activity?"

Vlad rubbed the back of his neck, deep in thought. After a few moments, he nodded. "It looks that way. I remember Avery was terrified of him."

Alessandra crossed her arms, lips pursed. "He's probably well-hidden and heavily guarded. Any chance these symbols can point us to him?"

Ash bent down, examining the intricate shapes carved into the stone floor. He ran his fingers along each glyph and muttered something under his breath. After a few minutes, he shook his head. "No. It seems to be some type of spell for locating and travelling to their master. Lord Darmon, I assume. But it requires blood to activate, so I doubt we could replicate it."

Lucien's words were barely audible as he inquired, "Are you implying that she might be beyond my reach?"

Vlad responded, "When I last spoke to her, she appeared to have accepted her fate as her father's minion and was aware that she would see him again, despite me confining her here. It's almost as if she saw it coming."

Lucien's voice trembled. "Uncle, you share a blood connection with her. Can't we use demonic magic to bring her back?"

Ash's response was firm. "That's not how our

magic operates. My son would need to be a demonic being for that to be possible, and I don't condone sacrificing one life to save another. It never ends well."

Lucien's brows furrowed, his frustration simmering just beneath the surface. He clenched his fists, his knuckles turning white as he struggled to contain his mounting anger. His eyes bore into the figure before him. The room grew tense, filled with an uncomfortable silence, until Lucien could no longer hold back.

With a sudden burst of emotion, his voice crackled with anger as he blurted out, "Then what's the point of you even being here, demon? You have done nothing to assist me in retrieving Avery."

The words hung heavily in the air, each syllable infused with his frustration and disappointment. His voice wavered with disbelief and defiance, his body language mirroring his internal turmoil. The room seemed to vibrate with the intensity of his outburst, and the weight of his words resonated with his genuine confusion and a touch of desperation.

Vlad intervened to calm the tense atmosphere between the two. "Let's not let this turn into a battle of words. We're all equally frustrated, searching for clues and trying to comprehend this situation. I don't think my father is to blame. Jade, what are your thoughts? Avery seemed to gaze in your direction."

"I don't believe she saw me. Rather, I think she knew I would come to this cell and that its memory would preserve her last moments here. She glanced at the box, then back at us, showing that she wants us to continue the fight against the Order. My intuition tells me that this map could be the key to finding her."

The group found themselves suddenly released from the memory spell as a soft light enveloped them.

"Let's rest and start again tomorrow," Alessandra said, taking Vlad's arm as they made their way towards the exit.

"Agreed," Ash chimed in, supporting Jade in assisting the still-traumatised Lucien.

As THEY SETTLED INTO THEIR CHAMBER, Alessandra turned to Vlad, her expression questioning. "You're keeping something from the others, aren't you?" she probed.

"You'll have to be more specific. I keep many things from people," Vlad responded, his attention shifting towards Alessandra. He helped her out of her clothes before escorting her to the bathroom, where he filled the tub with steaming water for them both.

Alessandra turned to find Vlad in the doorway, his gaze locked onto her.

"Don't play games. You know what I'm referring to," Alessandra pressed.

She held Vlad's gaze as he disrobed and slipped into the water beside her. The latent desire between them charged the air, though neither made a move.

"Do I?" he murmured, his voice low and heated.

She splayed her fingers across his bare chest, conflicting emotions churning within. Grief and confusion over Avery still gripped her heart, yet Vlad's proximity intoxicated her senses. She tingled with temptation, aching to give in, but hesitation held her back. His nearness was a bittersweet torture, pleasure and anguish intertwined.

"You noticed my slight hesitation," he continued. "You and Ash know me better than anyone else. I didn't want Lucien to run off in that state after her. When I saw her being taken away, I tried to use our blood connection. She's being held in another realm, or worse, dead."

"Thank you for protecting my brother, my love." She gazed at him through hooded eyes and whispered, "My prince."

"Anything for you, Alessa." He pulled her closer and kissed her soft lips, the water splashing around them. After a few moments, Alessandra pulled away.

"It's unlikely that Lord Darmon killed his own daughter," she continued. "It's more likely that she's his puppet, following his orders like his other minions."

"But what if she's in a different realm? Can our powerful witch track people in other realms?" Vlad asked.

"No." She shook her head. "But I know someone who can move between them with relative ease. My father."

"Then we shall find your father," Vlad declared, his eyes smouldering with unspoken intensity. He drew nearer, radiating heat, and seized her waist to pull her firmly against him. His kiss was feverish, fervent, belying his stoic restraint.

When he finally broke away, his hands trembled as they cradled her face. "God, I thought I'd lost you today," he rasped. Before she could respond, his mouth claimed hers once more, desperate to convey what words could not.

She yielded to his fervour, letting his passion sweep away the residual fear that had gripped them both. Enveloped in his arms, the terrors of the day melted away. There was only this—the warmth of his skin, the hammering of his heart matching her own. No more words were needed. For now, after coming so close to losing everything, this was enough.

Chapter 2

The tranquil Victorian garden provided a refuge for Alessandra. She sat on a rustic wooden bench that had been carved from a single piece of dark-stained wood. The gentle sounds of the fountain's cascading waters and the sweet floral scents that wafted through the air enveloped her in a soothing embrace, easing her troubled mind.

As she inhaled deeply, the delicate fragrance of

the blooming flowers carried her away to a place of peace and tranquillity. Gazing into the shimmering depths of the fountain, she watched as a solitary leaf floated by the calm waters. A small frog leaped from one lily pad to another, its nimble movements barely making a ripple on the serene surface.

Looking up to the starry sky, Alessandra basked in the comforting hug of the cool breeze that gently brushed against her skin. With closed eyes, she let her mind wander, losing herself in the moment until her thoughts faded, bringing clarity and calm. Alessandra felt confident that she could take on any challenge that her future held for her.

Suddenly, a new presence interrupted her peaceful daydream, causing Alessandra to startle. “It’s you,” she uttered, recognising the familiar figure.

Ash appeared before her with a playful chuckle. “Did you put my son to sleep and go wandering around the academy?”

Alessandra’s gaze softened as she thought of the vampire who was slumbering in their chamber, a behaviour that astonished her. “Maybe. He’s been sleeping much more recently. I wouldn’t have thought it was possible for his kind.”

Ash’s mouth curled into a knowing smile. “Your

blood is special and makes him more human," he said, his deep voice calm. She nodded in agreement and Ash continued, "Plus, there's this thing called love. Worries seem to fade away when you're close to someone you love. He's more content than I've seen him in centuries."

Alessandra sighed. "He will not be too happy tomorrow." She grimaced, understanding the reality of the situation despite how hard it was to accept it.

"You're leaving," Ash stated.

Again, she nodded her head in confirmation. Her mind reeled with all the ways things could go wrong if he joined her on her quest to find her father—a path filled with danger from members of the Order who wanted to use her against Vlad.

"I have to go look for my father, and taking the Order's most sought-after vampire away from the academy is not a wise choice. He'll want to come, but I can't risk his life. I'm the chink in his armour now. The Order will use me as bait."

"Take me instead. I may not have my full strength yet, but I'll do what I can to help you out," Ash offered.

Jade interjected with a wide grin as she appeared behind them. "A road trip? Count me in!"

Alessandra jumped and let out a breathy chuckle. "You scared me!" She gestured her open hands towards the two of them. "Both of you are welcome to come along if you don't give me a heart attack."

Ash rolled his eyes and lightly teased, "I thought assassins weren't supposed to be scaredy-cats. I'm not so impressed."

Alessandra bowed mockingly with her palms pressed together as if begging for mercy. "My deepest apologies, Your Highness. Must have forgotten my assassin hat from your son's chamber."

Jade snickered while Ash gave her an unamused side glance.

Moments later, Ash clapped his hands together and exclaimed, "It looks like we're going to get along famously! Let's not wait around until your overprotective boyfriend wakes up and impedes our fun."

They all shared a laugh at the thought of Vlad sending them to their own rooms.

"That is the cost of me going out with the headmaster, I suppose." Alessandra smiled at the thought of Vlad. She cherished him too much to risk any harm coming to him, so the best decision for them both was for her to leave him at the academy.

"To find out where my father is now, we must return to Bath. It holds special meaning for him and is where we shared many of our happiest moments."

"Do you want me to leave a message for when Vlad wakes up?" Jade inquired. "Think of a message you'd like to leave for him, and it will be visible when he wakes up."

Alessandra's heart pounded as she tried to decide how to tell Vlad the news. She was certain he would be furious, but she felt it was her responsibility to keep him safe from the Order, who were notorious for their merciless behaviour towards supernatural creatures. Though Alessandra had never considered herself brave, the thought of not being with Vlad brought tears to her eyes, and she courageously spoke up.

"All set. I just hope he will forgive me. What should I do now?" she asked Jade.

"Concentrate on that image while I cast a spell," Jade replied.

Alessandra obeyed and watched as the witch worked her magic. Once done, Jade flashed a smile at Alessandra.

"Vlad will someday forgive you. He holds an old-fashioned belief that he should be the one to rescue the damsel in distress. However, I'm confident that with your guidance, he'll move past this mindset. You're a total badass, and you don't need anyone else to overcome obstacles."

"All right, let's get this started. Everyone, join hands," Jade instructed. "Since I've already been to Bath, I can teleport us there with my spell. But I'll need your help, Alessandra, for the rest of the way."

"Got it," she replied, nodding.

"This is such a lovely feeling," Ash remarked. "We're already holding hands like best friends."

"Does he always talk nonsense?" Alessandra laughed.

"Quiet, Ash," Jade scolded him. "I need to focus on the spell." Turning to Alessandra, she added, "You have no idea."

Ash jumped in, protesting, "Hey, I'm still here, ladies." His eyebrows furrowed in annoyance.

With a hushed incantation, Jade enveloped them in magic. In a blink, the scene shifted to a shadowy Bath alley, cramped between looming buildings. The narrow path twisted ahead like a maze, illuminated only by the weak flicker of streetlamps. Their pallid light cast the uneven cobblestones in odd, disorienting shadows.

As Alessandra looked around, she noticed the walls were made of weathered brick, and in some places, ivy grew up the sides, clinging to the rough, uneven surfaces. The air was thick with a faint mist, which added to the surreal and otherworldly atmosphere of the alleyway. It was as though someone had transported them to a different time and place. The only sound that could be heard was the distant mewling of a cat, lending an air of ominous stillness to the surroundings.

As they stood there, Alessandra felt a sense of uneasiness creeping over her. It was as though the alleyway held a secret. Something they were not meant to discover.

"Hey, if this doesn't pan out, remind me to take you monster hunting so we can make some money as mercenaries," Alessandra said, trying to break the looming silence.

"Ha, don't worry! With us together, no beast will be safe." Jade chuckled.

"Don't forget about me either." Ash fluttered his eyelashes.

"I thought you'd want to do something with the boys?" Jade smiled.

"I'm all about adventure, not like the other two," Ash joked.

"Let's get back to business. We still have to figure out where we are and how we can get to my old home without being spotted by the Order," Alessandra commanded.

"Before that, tell us which magical place from your childhood we're going to visit," Ash demanded with a raised eyebrow.

"Ah, sorry about that. It's called Prior Park Mansion. It's been in my family's possession for quite some time, although it had to be rebuilt twice due to it burning down."

"Wow, I didn't know your family was so well-off," Jade exclaimed in surprise.

"We don't talk about it."

Jade's excitement was palpable as she spoke. "I can't believe you had a butler. I'm getting Sebastian vibes."

Ash raised an eyebrow at Jade's enthusiasm. "What's the big deal about a butler?" he inquired. "And who's this Sebastian guy? Is he some playboy you've been seeing before me?"

Alessandra rolled her eyes at Ash's assumption. "No, Ash. He's not a real person. Jade is just excited because the butler reminds her of a character from an anime she loves."

Jade nodded. "Yeah, he's like my childhood crush come to life."

After Jade's admission, Ash pulled out his phone and scrolled through a few images before speaking. "Hm, you have good taste." He paused for a moment before speaking again. "You know I can change into any form, right? I can make all your fantasies come to life," he added with a mischievous grin.

"I don't think I want to hear this," Alessandra replied, her voice tight with unease. She couldn't shake off the feeling that something was watching them.

"Are you sure they're watching your house, or are you taking your role as an assassin too seriously?" Ash asked.

Alessandra felt a tinge of anger at his remark. She had worked hard to become who she was today, and it wasn't just a game to her. But she pushed it down and reminded herself that he was just trying to lighten the mood.

With a deep breath, she forced a smile and responded confidently, "I'm certain. But that won't stop us from getting the job done."

"I've dealt with their kind before, but I never thought they'd be so vicious," Ash confessed.

Alessandra's heart pounded as Ash spoke. Memories of gruelling, cruel training flooded her mind, but she refused to let fear show on her face. She straightened her back and summoned bravery.

"Same here. I feel like I've been burying my head in the sand when it comes to them. I feel bad for you, Alessandra," Jade sympathised.

"No need to pity me," she replied, her voice steady. "I was born into this, so I knew what I was getting myself into. It's all new to you guys, and that's the hard part."

As she spoke, her mind raced with images of countless battles fought, lives taken. But instead of crumbling, she pushed emotions aside and focused on the task at hand. The night air hung heavy, silent as they walked, but she stayed grateful for the darkness that hid threatening tears.

A wrought-iron gate, which creaked ominously in the gentle breeze, marked the entrance to the neighbouring cemetery. The group stepped inside, their footsteps echoing through the graveyard. Headstones were scattered haphazardly, some of them centuries old.

"We have to be quiet here," Alessandra

murmured. "They train the knights to recognise unusual sounds, so no sudden noises."

"I may have a solution for that, unless they have a witch of their own," Jade replied, then gestured with her hands. An enormous bubble enveloped the trio, muffling all sound.

The night fog had descended upon them like a heavy silken blanket. They strolled down the lane from the main entrance of the old, forgotten chapel. Mist only added to the eerie atmosphere, making it increasingly terrifying with every step. Bare trees surrounded the cemetery, twisted branches reaching like skeletal fingers. An owl's occasional hoot was the only sound they could hear.

As the group walked along the path, the shadows appeared to follow them, creating a haunting orchestra of dark shapes in the air. Now and then, they observed the weathered gravestones that lined the way, seeking solace in the hush. However, the chapel ahead was even more daunting.

Moss encrusted the aged walls of the building, and its stained-glass windows depicted tales of death and hopelessness. They could feel the weight of time upon them, as if the fog was concealing more sinister things lurking nearby.

Alessandra's keen ears perked up, and her senses tingled with an inexplicable awareness. The faint sound that emanated from the chapel was unlike anything she had heard before—an ethereal melody that seemed to transcend the boundaries of reality.

As she listened, the world around her seemed to blur, the bustling city fading into the background as if they had been transported to a different realm. Time lost its grip, and seconds stretched into moments that held no significance. It was as though they were suspended in a realm of magic and enchantment. Alessandra's heart quickened, and she exchanged a bewildered glance with her companions. None of them desired to enter, but it was the only way to the mansion undetected by the Order.

The group hesitantly pushed open the door and the surrounding fog dissipated like smoke. Inside the chapel, the air was still and heavy, as if it held the secrets of the past. The walls were adorned with dark paintings, and candles flickered, casting eerie shadows on the ground. As they walked down the aisle, Alessandra couldn't help but feel as if she was trespassing into a forbidden world. However, their mission was too important to back down now. They had to get to the mansion without raising suspicions.

From the shadows of the chapel, a voice resounded, "Welcome." Jade ceased her spell to muffle sounds since their presence was already exposed. Alessandra had no clue who the speaker could be, as it wasn't her father or any known Order member.

With growing frustration, Alessandra raised her voice, "Reveal yourself. I am not here to play games. Are you an ally or an enemy?"

The voice responded with an eerie laugh that sent shivers down her spine. The group shared a glance, confirming their need to prepare for a fight. Ash summoned his sapphire-coloured flames, setting the stone floor ablaze to illuminate the area.

The Hellfire burned with a fierce intensity, casting an ominous blue glow over the chapel. The light revealed every detail of the ornate architecture, from the towering stone arches to the intricate gold inlays, giving the room an otherworldly ambiance.

From a shadowed corner a cloaked figure emerged, its movements slow and deliberate. The heavy fabric of the cloak rustled like restless spirits as it approached the fire, pausing for a moment as if contemplating a weighty decision. Leaning forward, the mysterious individual whispered something into the flames, the words so low and faint that no one else could hear them.

Silently, the enigmatic presence stepped away from the fire and vanished into the darkness, leaving the mystery of its whispered secret to be kept by the flames. For a fleeting moment, the air hung still with an unsettling silence until the flames flickered and vanished, shrouding the chapel in darkness, with only the faint glow of the moon outside providing any light.

The passage of time seemed suspended in that instant, leaving those who bore witness with a profound sense of awe and unease. It was as if the chapel itself had held its breath, patiently awaiting the figure to reveal its secret before exhaling and withdrawing into the shadows once more.

Chapter 7

ALESSANDRA REGARDED ASH'S EVIDENT disappointment with a mix of empathy and amusement. She knew he had been itching for combat, and the standoff with the mysterious cloaked man had only whetted his appetite for action. Though Ash now seemed frustrated at the anticlimactic outcome, Alessandra felt a swell of relief that the encounter hadn't turned violent.

Her musings were broken off by Ash's voice. "That was strange," he grumbled. "I was hungry for a fight."

She couldn't help but giggle at his eagerness. "The night still has plenty in store," she stated. "Whoever, or whatever that was, it put out your fire. I didn't think that could be done."

Ash's aspect grew more serious as he replied, "You're correct. My Hellfire is special; it comes from my soul so no other prince of Hell can control it. Yet a duke of Hell has the power to snuff it out with no effort at all. It wasn't wise for us to face him directly."

Alessandra contemplated Ash's explanation, trying to comprehend the magnitude of this stranger's abilities. She could not ignore the feeling that there was more to this enigmatic figure than they imagined.

"Just so I understand this correctly," Jade chimed in. "Are princes lower ranked than dukes down in Hell?"

Alessandra couldn't help but roll her eyes at Jade's query. "Yes, princes are lower ranked than dukes," she verified. "It's basic demonology."

Ash responded, "Hell isn't 'down there'. It is on a different plane, parallel to all the others."

The assassin grinned. "I'll keep that in mind for my next demonology quiz."

Their humorous exchange came to an abrupt end when Alessandra's instincts kicked in. "Hold up," she announced, raising her hand to pause them. "I have a bad feeling about this."

Just then, a voice echoed through the chapel, causing them to startle. "You should listen to your gut instinct, Alessandra," the voice uttered. It was the same creepy voice from before, now coming from inside their heads.

Jade stepped forward and lit the strategically placed braziers around the area. When the chapel glowed brightly, the figure reappeared, but this time it kept changing its form.

"Who are you?" Alessandra demanded.

"I am Azaroth, the demon with a thousand faces. It is a pleasure to meet you at last," he replied in a soothing voice.

"What do you desire from us?" she inquired, her heart pounding in her chest.

Azaroth laughed before his form shifted again. "I ask for nothing from you, my dear. I only wish to watch and see what the great assassin of the Order can do."

Alessandra gritted her teeth together as she

heard this. Azaroth was trying to manipulate them, but she didn't know how to fight back against an entity with so many forms and powers.

The demon changed shape again, taking on the image of Alessandra's father. She gasped and stepped away from him in surprise.

"Come join me, my daughter," Azaroth spoke in her father's voice. "Together we can rule over the Order, all of Hell, and more."

Alessandra's eyes narrowed as she realised what was happening. The demon was trying to use her love for her father against her. She dropped to the floor, her hands trembling as she pulled out a dagger hidden in the top of her right boot. Her assassin training had taught her not to hesitate, but when she saw the demon with her father's face, it was like a stillness descended on her. She shook off the shock and swung at the creature with all her might.

Moonlight flashed off her dagger as she hurled it, spinning, at the demon. She ducked under raking claws, their fiery heat scalding the air above her. Lunging in, she stabbed at its chest but the creature skittered back, evading the blow. She circled, seeking an opening, but its speed matched her own. Again and again they collided, blade glancing off scales, claws narrowly missing flesh - a deadly dance with neither able to strike true.

Jade and Ash advanced with purposeful strides. Yet, as they neared the menacing demon, an unseen and formidable force propelled them backward. Their bodies staggered, their momentum abruptly halted. The proximity to Alessandra, locked in a fierce battle with the demonic entity, felt insurmountable. A pulsating wall of impenetrable energy materialised, creating a dividing barrier.

Frustration and anguish etched their faces as Jade and Ash relentlessly pounded their fists against the barrier. Their actions conveyed a profound message, a visual portrayal of their desperate desire to aid their friend. Each blow reverberated, echoing their steadfast tenacity to surmount the obstacle and reach Alessandra's side. The demon's laughter echoed throughout the chamber as if it were mocking their attempts. Alessandra looked over at them and shook her head, signalling that they should stay back. Defeated, the couple backed away from the barrier.

"Your tricks won't work on me, demon," Alessandra yelled as she parried a ferocious attack.

The demon's laugh turned silken as his form morphed again, adopting the guise of a striking man. Silver hair cascaded over broad shoulders, framing a sculpted face. But it was the eyes that gave Alessandra pause—brilliant emerald pools belying ancient cunning. She steadied her grip, wary of the predatory intelligence watching her every move.

"Is this more to your liking, my dear assassin? I hear you have a thing for pretty monsters."

As she recalled her demand for answers, her eyes bore into him with an icy intensity. The edges of her lips curved downward, and her hands were clenched into tight fists. "I asked you a question. Is there a reason you're toying with us? Ash told me who you are. We could all be dead by now if you wanted. So, tell me, what's your game?"

The demon roared with fury and pushed Alessandra to the ground with a single shove. He then advanced towards the illuminated barrier that was sectioning the room, his eyes blazing a trail of fire towards Ash.

"Asmodeus," he snarled. "I see you are running around with an assassin from the Order and a mighty witch. Quite curious indeed. Why have you forsaken your post in the abyss?"

Ash, better known as Asmodeus in Hell, took a step forward, his gaze unwavering from the demon.

He looked at Alessandra, silently instructing her to stay down. "I didn't forsake my post." He spoke calmly, despite the rage emanating from the other demon. "I merely took a detour."

Azaroth, still in his handsome form, threw his head back in laughter. "A detour, you say?" His laughter subsided as he took a step closer towards the barrier. "I've been waiting for you to slip up, Asmodeus. You were always quite the thorn in my side in Hell."

"What do you mean?"

Azaroth laughed. "You are Lucifer's little obedient soldier, wouldn't you agree? Why do you think you've been summoned out of Hell so often? It's all been down to a little help from me. And when you return—and trust me, you will—your followers will notice that stench on you. The stench of human feelings, love, etc. You're a changed demon now, Asmodeus. You're not worthy of ever returning to the pit."

Ash's features hardened at Azaroth's taunting words. His eyes, full of mischief, now radiated a deadly seriousness. He clenched his fists, the air around him buzzing with latent power. "I am no one's soldier," he retorted, "And my worthiness is not for you to judge."

"And as for my 'stench'..." His lips twisted into a snarl. "At least I'm not a coward hiding behind illusions."

Azaroth's lips curled in icy amusement. "Such harsh words, Asmodeus," he purred, tone laden with false affability. "I'd hoped we could chat cordially, like old friends. But it seems you've forgotten your place."

"I have forgotten nothing," Ash shot back. "Especially not your penchant for deceit."

The room's atmosphere was a powder keg ready to detonate. Alessandra and Jade observed the standoff with bated breath, neither daring to speak. This was a viper's nest, and any sudden moves could mean disaster.

Just as it seemed the tension could not get any higher, Azaroth broke into a fit of laughter, the sound echoing off the chapel walls. "Oh, Asmodeus." He cackled. "You've always been too serious for your own good. I am nothing more than a spectator enjoying the minor war between some tiny creatures and the Order. Do you think the organisation has got where they are by being a force of good?"

"So, what do you want from us? What's your play? Are you here to help or hinder?" Alessandra asked.

Azaroth's laughter faded as he turned his gaze to Alessandra. "Help or hinder? Such binary thinking, dear assassin," he chided. "The world isn't divided into black and white, good and evil."

Alessandra gripped her dagger tighter, her knuckles turning white. "You're avoiding the question," she countered, her voice steady.

Azaroth let out a nonchalant shrug. "What I want is immaterial. It's what you want that matters, Alessandra," he said, his voice dropping low. "What are you willing to do to protect your friends? To ensure their survival against the Order? Are you ready to spill blood, even if it's your own?"

Alessandra fought to keep her composure as she swallowed hard. In all her years as an assassin, she had never crossed paths with a foe like Azaroth before. His every word was deliberately chosen and laced with menace. Though icy fear churned within her, Alessandra stood tall and did not retreat. She had confronted countless threats in the past and survived. She would not let this demon, dire as he was, shake her resolve. Gathering her courage, she met his serpentine gaze directly.

"What I want is for you to leave. To stop interfering in matters that don't concern you," she shot back, her gaze unwavering.

Azaroth let out a slow, appreciative clap. "Bravo, Alessandra. So much spirit." His gaze hardened as he looked back at Asmodeus. "As for you, old friend, it seems your brief detour has changed you more than you think. You're no longer the demon I knew. Your time among humans has... softened you."

Ash, who had been observing the exchange, stepped forward, his eyes glowing with an inner fire. "And you're just as manipulative and deceitful as always, Azaroth. Your games end here."

Ash's gaze connected with Jade's, who had abruptly materialised by his side, prompting him to grasp her hand firmly. United in their powers, they held onto a glimmer of hope.

"Indeed," Jade confirmed, her grip on Ash's hand growing tighter. The atmosphere crackled with electric anticipation as they intertwined their abilities. Their fused magic crafted an intricate tapestry of vibrant power, casting a radiant glow throughout the chapel's sombre interior.

Jade and Ash raised their unoccupied hands, their fingertips aglow with amassed strength. Bound by unending willpower, they unleashed a surge of energy, colliding it head-on with Azaroth. The rush of mystical force surged through the air, causing braziers to flicker and the stones of the chapel to quiver under its sheer might.

Azaroth hissed, his form rippling as he sought to evade the incoming assault. Yet the merged prowess of Jade and Ash persisted relentlessly and swiftly. The blast struck Azaroth with unrelenting vigour, evoking a shrill cry of agony that reverberated through the chapel.

Alessandra sprinted forward, her dagger held high. Azaroth was recoiling from Jade and Ash's attack, his attention on them. He didn't see Alessandra until it was too late. With a battle cry, she plunged her dagger into Azaroth.

Silence gripped the room as Azaroth hovered, wavering on the brink. Then, with an anguished howl, the demon erupted in a blast of power, his body bursting apart and dissipating like mist.

Alessandra reeled back, chest heaving, her fingers numb around the hilt of her fallen dagger. Beside her, Jade and Ash slumped breathless to their knees, utterly depleted. For a long moment, none of them stirred, too shaken to grasp what had happened.

Chapter 4

GASPING FOR BREATH, ALESSANDRA LAY COLLAPSED as her mind spun wildly. Azaroth's cryptic words lingered, their implications obscure yet demanding. Had the demon's verbal snares held any truth, or were they only more deception?

His layered taunts needled her thoughts. The allusions to the Order, Asmodeus, herself—they formed a puzzle with missing pieces. One she struggled to assemble into meaning.

With ruthless skill, Azaroth had scattered partial facts and veiled threats, delighting in misdirection. But Alessandra sensed some greater strategy underpinning it all. She strained to discern the larger picture, to unravel the demon's designs.

"What did he mean, Ash?" Alessandra inquired, turning her gaze to the demon, who was trying to recover his strength. "Why did he say that you were 'a changed demon'?"

Ash's eyes flickered open. He looked at Alessandra, his gaze heavy. "He was just trying to get under my skin," he dismissed, his voice raspy. "It's what he does best. We shouldn't read too much into his words."

Alessandra remained unconvinced. She knew Ash was trying to brush it off to avoid the topic. But Azaroth had been too interested in their affairs for it to be just random talk. There was something more. Alessandra had a sinking feeling that they were only scratching the surface of a much larger problem.

"Are you sure about that?" she pressed. "You knew him before, didn't you? What if there's some truth in what he said? What if there is a bigger threat to the Order?"

The silence that followed was heavy. They had won the battle, but a sense of unease lingered. As the adrenaline of the fight drained away, they were left knowing that their struggle was far from over. Azaroth might be gone, but his shadow still loomed over them, a reminder that dangers still lurked in the darkness.

Alessandra got up from the floor, then pulled the other two up. "Let's not dwell on it. For all I know, he could've been the Order's dog, placed at the entrance to the secret tunnel. We're here to find clues to my father's whereabouts, so let's do just that."

Guiding orb aloft, Ash led them further within. Ancient air hung heavy, their footfalls rousing dust motes to dance in the pale light. Though eerie, a sense of stillness pervaded the chapel's heart, untouched by their battle. There was something hallowed here, eternal. Shadows could not mar the steadfast sanctity of this place.

Scanning the room, Alessandra found various symbols etched into the stone walls, faded but still discernible. Some were emblems she recognised from her training with the Order, others were unfamiliar, belonging perhaps to ancient sects or old magic.

Alessandra's breath caught as her gaze fell upon a familiar sigil - one intricately linked to her father. An eminent dragon formed the emblem's centrepiece, scales gleaming in deep emerald and crimson, wings spread in a display of formidable power. Sharp talons clutched an ornate sword, grasping the hilt with undeniable authority.

Surrounding the dragon, elaborate runic patterns and arcane symbols adorned the edges like an ancient tapestry. Each intricate curve seemed to thrum with energy, resonating within Alessandra's spirit. The sigil evoked her father's tales of mythic battles and forgotten realms now lost to time.

Significance was attached to the colours of the emblem too. The vibrant green symbolised growth, renewal, and the ever-present connection to nature. The fiery red evoked passion, courage, and the unyielding spirit that ran through her bloodline.

As she stared at the image, a mix of emotions washed over her—pride, longing, and a burning desire to uncover the truth behind her father's legacy. It served as a reminder of the weight of responsibility that came with it.

Now, with the emblem before her, she felt a

surge of determination. Alessandra took a deep breath, ready to step into the unknown and embrace the challenges that awaited her.

"We're on the right path," she said, her voice a whisper, her gaze intense.

A radiant light beckoned from the passage's depths, flowing from an ornately carved altar nestled in the chamber beyond. Intricate symbols and arcane script adorned the walls, their significance gradually revealing itself. As she drew nearer, Alessandra traced the elegant engravings, once shrouded in shadow now limned in luminescence.

With bated breath, Alessandra, Jade, and Ash shared a knowing glance. They had come too far to turn back now. Together, they stepped further into the altar room. Their eyes were immediately drawn to a stunning painting that hung on the wall. The vibrant colours and elaborate details captured their attention, but it was the subject of the painting that left Alessandra breathless.

It was her mother, lovingly rendered in exquisite detail. The artist had truly captured her gentle spirit, reflecting the warmth and compassion Alessandra cherished in her fading memories.

She approached with trembling steps, overcome with a flood of emotion. This painting was more than a mere image—it radiated her mother's very essence. Alessandra reached out a quivering hand, fingers gently tracing the brushstrokes. In that fleeting contact, she felt profoundly connected, as if her mother was right there, watchful eyes brimming with affection.

Bittersweet longing pierced Alessandra's heart. Here was the one she had lost yet loved so dearly, preserved in timeless splendour. The beauty of the portrait stirred joy at this glimpse of her mother's graceful soul. Yet it also brought deep sorrow at the permanence of her absence. Tears blurred Alessandra's vision as she beheld the painting. It answered none of her questions, only deepening the hollow ache of missing her family. But in rediscovering her mother's comforting presence, she found unexpected solace tinged with pain.

In front of the painting, Alessandra broke down, her tears cascading down her cheeks as she mourned the loss of her mother once again.

Jade and Ash stood by her side, their own eyes filled with empathy and understanding. They offered a comforting presence, allowing Alessandra the space she needed to release her grief. A tender silence filled the room, only interrupted by the sound of Alessandra's soft sobs.

As the weight of her emotions eased, Alessandra wiped away her tears and took a deep breath. Though her heart ached, she drew strength from the love she shared with her mother and the memory of her presence. She rose to her feet, a renewed fortitude shining in her eyes.

"I'm so sorry, guys. I didn't mean to break down like that."

Jade placed a comforting hand on Alessandra's shoulder. "Hey, there's no need to apologise. We understand. Finding this place, it's a deeply emotional moment for you."

"Absolutely, Alessandra," Ash chipped in. "And if you want to talk about it, I'm a superb listener. Thousands of years in Hell listening to all those souls whine about how their death was unfair gives a demon a lot of perspective."

Jade rolled her eyes. "You had to ruin it, didn't you?"

Alessandra couldn't help but chuckle through her lingering tears. "You two are something else. Even amid my breakdown, you make me laugh."

Jade shook her head, a small smile playing on her lips. "Well, what are friends for if not to bring a little humour into the mix, even in the toughest of times?"

Ash dramatically placed a hand over his heart, feigning a wounded expression. "Ah, my tragic existence. Misunderstood by all, except for my dear friend Alessandra."

Alessandra playfully rolled her eyes. "Oh, please. Don't get too carried away now, Ash. Let's focus on the task at hand."

Jade nodded in agreement. "He's right, though. We're here for you, Alessandra. Through the laughter and the tears, we've got your back."

Alessandra's gratitude overflowed. She squeezed Jade's hand and smiled at Ash's theatrical display. "Thank you both. I'm lucky to have friends like you. Now, let's take a deep breath, wipe away these tears, and continue on our journey. We have mysteries to unravel and a destiny to fulfil."

Ash straightened his posture. "Indeed, my lady. Onward we shall march, facing danger and adventure with style and charm."

Jade rolled her eyes once again but couldn't hide her amusement. "Oh, Ash, always the showman. But you're right, Alessandra. Together, we're a formidable trio. We'll face whatever comes our way and come out stronger on the other side."

Alessandra's heart swelled with gratitude. She knew she was not alone in her quest. With Jade and

Ash by her side, she felt invincible. Their friendship was a beacon of light in the darkness that surrounded them.

As Alessandra, Jade, and Ash entered the next room, a chilling draft filled the air, sending a shiver down their spines. The chamber was engulfed in an eerie darkness, illuminated by flickering torches that cast dancing shadows on the ancient walls.

The door behind them slammed shut, sealing them inside. Panic surged within Alessandra, but she remained resolute, knowing that she had to face whatever lay ahead.

As their eyes adjusted to the dim light, they noticed a series of detailed carvings etched into the walls, depicting menacing creatures of legend. The air grew heavier, and an ominous presence filled the room, as if unseen eyes were watching their every move.

A deep rumbling sound reverberated through the chamber, causing the floor beneath their feet to tremble. The carvings on the walls came alive, transforming into ethereal manifestations of the creatures they depicted. The once motionless figures now moved with eerie fluidity, their eyes glowing with an unsettling light.

Alessandra's heart raced as she realised they

were facing the guardians of the chamber. The mystical entities, trapped for centuries, woke up because of their presence and intended to test their worthiness.

With a bone-chilling howl that reverberated through the chamber, the first guardian lunged forward, propelled by an otherworldly force, its monstrous claws extended and poised for a devastating strike. Alessandra's heart raced in her chest as she, Jade, and Ash moved in perfect synchrony, their actions a testament to their shared determination and honed abilities. She braced herself, ready to confront the imminent threat.

In a display of agility and speed, they gracefully evaded the razor-sharp claws, countering with calculated precision. Their movements flowed seamlessly, a well-practiced choreography that showcased their tenacity. Every swing of her weapon, every nimble dodge, ignited a fire within Alessandra, reinforcing her belief that they were capable of facing any challenge.

However, the guardians' embodiments of darkness and malevolence proved to be more than mere opponents. The very room seemed to pulse with their nefarious power, magnifying their strength. Shadows writhed and contorted, giving birth to insidious tendrils that slithered across the floor, ensnaring their limbs in a vice-like grip. Each constriction threatened to immobilise them, testing their resilience and fortitude.

Despite the encroaching darkness, Alessandra refused to succumb. Alongside Jade and Ash, she fought back, their spirits unyielding. She summoned every ounce of strength, pushing beyond her limits, determined to break free from the suffocating grasp of the shadowy restraints. With each struggle, every defiant motion, they defied the insidious influence seeking to bind them.

This was another sign that they were getting closer to finding the whereabouts of her father. Only he would think to protect his legacy with dark magic.

As oppressive darkness smothered the chamber, Alessandra's steadfastness blazed defiantly. She now grasped that these shadow guardians were more than just physical foes—they embodied her father's mystical might.

Drawing upon her inner strength, Alessandra tapped into the latent power that had always been a part of her. She focused her mind and summoned a brilliant aura of light that radiated from her core, pushing back the encroaching gloom.

Jade and Ash, sensing her unwavering resolve, followed suit, channelling their own unique abilities. Jade's agility and precision became a whirlwind of energy, cutting through the shadowy tendrils that threatened to ensnare them. Ash, with his affinity for manipulating fire, conjured blazing flames that licked at the shadows, driving them back.

Together, they fought against the guardians, their unity a beacon of light in the face of darkness. Alessandra couldn't help but feel a bittersweet mix of emotions. On one hand, she resented her father for the challenges he had left in his wake. But she couldn't deny the connection that drew her closer to him with each passing trial.

As they continued their relentless assault, the guardians grew weaker, their dark energy waning. The room trembled, and cracks formed on the walls, releasing a blinding light that shattered the remaining shadows.

In the battle's aftermath, Alessandra's heart swelled with emotions. She had come one step closer to uncovering the truth about her father, his motives, and his role in the mysterious events that had shaped her life.

Chapter 5

EMERGING FROM THE CHAPEL'S TWISTING PASSAGES, the trio found themselves in an expansive chamber awash in the moonlight's otherworldly glow. Alessandra's pulse quickened as recognition dawned —this was the fabled place her father's tales had conjured. Its splendour stole the breath from her lungs.

The expansive chamber revealed a celestial

wonder above—a ceiling crafted entirely of toughened glass, allowing the soft lunar glow to cascade into the room. The shimmering beams danced across the chamber's walls, creating an ambiance that ignited a sense of wonder within their hearts.

Alessandra couldn't help but smile, her gaze fixated on the door standing proudly at the end of the hall. It was the very door her father had described—the entrance that would lead them into the long-awaited embrace of the mansion itself.

She felt a pang of nostalgia as she stepped into Prior Park mansion, her childhood home that had once been filled with warmth and laughter. Now it lay in decay, a haunting reminder of her father's mysterious disappearance.

The air inside was heavy with memories and neglect. Dust danced in the sunbeams that filtered through the cracked windows, casting an ethereal glow upon the worn wooden floors. Cobwebs clung to the corners, veiling the once elegant décor with a shroud of abandonment.

Every room she entered carried echoes of her past, triggering bittersweet emotions within her. The grand staircase, where she used to play and imagine glorious adventures, now sagged under the weight of time. The once vibrant wallpaper peeled from the walls, revealing faded remnants of a life she had long left behind.

In the old drawing room, Alessandra's gaze fell upon a portrait of her family, its frame tarnished and cracked. Her father's absence left an empty space in the composition, a painful reminder of the unanswered questions that plagued her.

As she ventured further, the mansion seemed to whisper its secrets. The creaking floorboards and the howling wind through the broken windows whispered of forgotten tales and unspoken truths. It was as if the very walls held the answers she sought, waiting for her to unravel the mysteries that lingered in every shadow.

With each step, she felt the weight of responsibility, the duty to reclaim the lost legacy of her family and uncover the truth behind her father's disappearance. The mansion became not only a physical labyrinth but also a representation of her own journey of self-discovery.

Alessandra's heart raced with anticipation as she explored the dilapidated corridors of the old mansion. The air was thick with dust and the musty scent of neglect, as if time itself had forgotten this place.

As she moved deeper into the labyrinthine maze

of forgotten rooms, a faint glimmer of hope ignited within her. She had heard whispers of her father's secret study, a sanctuary where he would immerse himself in ancient texts and delve into the mysteries that consumed him. It was said to hold the key to his knowledge, and perhaps it also had the answers she sought.

Her footsteps echoed through the abandoned halls, the sound a poignant reminder of the solitude she felt. The grandeur of the mansion had faded over the years, its once opulent decor now reduced to faded wallpaper and cracked marble. Yet, within these decaying walls, Alessandra sensed the lingering presence of her father, guiding her toward his hidden sanctuary.

With each step, her excitement grew, mingled with a tinge of trepidation. What secrets would she uncover in her father's study? What truths lay hidden among the ancient tomes and artefacts that adorned the room? Her mind whirled with possibilities as she moved closer to her destination.

Alessandra's steps halted at an aged oak door, its wood greyed and splintered from years untouched. The very air seemed alive with anticipation, as if the portal held its breath, poised on the cusp of revelation. She raised an unsteady hand, fingertips hovering above the tarnished brass knob. Her pulse thundered—a heady blend of eagerness and apprehension.

With a gentle twist, the door creaked open, revealing a dimly lit room bathed in a soft, golden glow. The air was heavy with the scent of aged parchment and the faint aroma of incense. As she stepped across the threshold, her eyes widened with wonder.

The chamber bore testament to her father's insatiable hunger for lost wisdom. Shelves stretched across the walls, bowed under the weight of leather-bound tomes, unrolled scrolls curling with age, and curios from faraway lands. Gold-leafed spines glinted in the sparse light, etched with glyphs from tongues long dead. Strange instruments of metal and glass cluttered tabletops, their arcane purposes veiled by dust and time.

Jade trailed closely behind, her presence a comforting reassurance. With a graceful flick of her wrist, she ignited the candles adorning the room. The warm glow of the flames illuminated the surroundings, casting mesmerising shadows that danced along the rows of books. The interplay of light and shadow seemed to breathe life into the stillness, as if the secrets within those ancient tomes yearned to be whispered into existence.

Upon entering, Alessandra's eyes were drawn to a large wooden desk cluttered with parchments and leather-bound volumes. The surface bore the marks of countless hours of meticulous study, ink stains and worn edges testifying to her father's tireless pursuit of understanding.

She approached the desk, running her fingers lightly over the worn wood, tracing the intricate carvings that adorned its surface. Emotions welled up within her—nostalgia, longing, and a deep sense of connection to her father. She could almost hear his voice, guiding her through the pages of knowledge that lay before her.

As she surveyed the room, Alessandra's eyes landed on a hidden alcove tucked away in the corner. It was a smaller space concealed behind an intricately woven tapestry that depicted scenes of mythical creatures and celestial beings. Something inside her urged her to investigate further.

With cautious steps, she approached the alcove and gently pushed aside the tapestry, revealing a hidden door. Its surface bore markings and symbols she recognised from her father's notes, confirming that this was the entrance to his most guarded sanctuary.

Her heart swelled with excitement and trepidation. She knew that beyond that door awaited the culmination of her father's knowledge, the secrets that could hold the key to understanding his disappearance and the mysteries that had plagued her. Taking a deep breath, she steeled herself for what lay ahead.

Alessandra reached out, her hand grasping the doorknob. She turned it. The door swung open, revealing a room bathed in an otherworldly glow. The walls were adorned with various symbols, and the air crackled with a sense of ancient power.

As she crossed the threshold into her father's hidden part of the study, a wave of emotions engulfed Alessandra—awe, wonder, and a profound sense of purpose. The room, steeped in an air of reverence, held the promise of unveiling the ambiguous truth that had eluded her for far too long. The arduous journey she had embarked upon had led her to this pivotal juncture, where she stood poised to embrace the profound knowledge that awaited her.

Alessandra, Jade, and Ash found themselves standing in her father's abandoned chamber, surrounded by a sea of forgotten books and dusty relics. Their eyes widened with curiosity as they surveyed the room, unsure of what peculiar surprises awaited them.

Alessandra's voice rang out with a touch of apprehension. "Ash, just a friendly reminder. Try to resist the urge to touch anything. We wouldn't want any ancient curses or angry spirits coming after us."

Ash flashed a mischievous grin, his eyes gleaming. "Oh, don't worry, Alessandra. I've been known to charm angry spirits with my irresistible wit. They can't resist a good joke!"

Jade rolled her eyes, trying to stifle a laugh. "Let's not tempt fate. Remember, we're here to solve mysteries, not become them."

Ash dramatically feigned offense, placing a hand over his heart. "Jade, you wound me! Here I am, just trying to add a little levity to this dusty situation."

Alessandra couldn't help but chuckle. "All right, Ash. Just remember that if you accidentally summon a ghost, you're in charge of making friends with it."

The trio shared a light-hearted laugh, momentarily forgetting the eerie atmosphere around them.

Alessandra knew that by delving into the depths

of his research, she would not only uncover his legacy, but also find the answers she sought. She took a deep breath, her eyes fixed on the vast expanse of knowledge that lay before her, ready to embark on a journey that would forever shape her destiny.

Hidden within the forgotten corners of the mansion, Alessandra's heart quickened as she stumbled upon remnants of her father's research. Scattered notes and weathered parchment hinted at his deep involvement in ancient mysteries and arcane knowledge, fuelling her curiosity and igniting a newfound sense of purpose.

The notes, written in her father's distinct handwriting, unveiled tantalising fragments of his journey. They spoke of his tireless pursuit of forbidden knowledge, and his relentless quest to uncover the secrets that lay beyond the veil of reality. Alessandra traced her fingers over the faded ink, absorbing the words as if they were a lifeline connecting her to her father's legacy.

As she pieced together the scattered puzzle, a tapestry of her father's discoveries emerged. Within the pages of ancient texts and forgotten lore, a wealth of knowledge awaited, unlocking insights into unseen realms, mystical artefacts brimming with untapped potential, and the existence of enigmatic beings that defied human comprehension.

Each note unravelled a layer of her father's obsession, painting a picture of a man driven by a desire to protect and preserve the delicate balance between worlds. His involvement in ancient mysteries extended far beyond mere curiosity—it was a calling, a sacred duty he had willingly embraced.

Alessandra's mind raced with questions and possibilities. She found diagrams detailing intricate rituals, sketches of enchanted artefacts, and references to ancient prophecies that foretold the coming of a great upheaval. Her father's research hinted at a world teetering on the brink of chaos, where dark forces conspired to disrupt the fragile harmony that held existence together.

These vestiges of her father's research were more than just remnants from a forgotten past; they were the breadcrumbs leading her closer to the truth. They fuelled her mission to continue his work, to understand the significance of his findings, and to carry the torch he had ignited.

With every page turned, Alessandra delved deeper into the enigmatic world her father had inhabited. She immersed herself in the complex tapestry of ancient myths and forbidden knowledge, determined to unravel the secrets that had driven her father's actions and, ultimately, shaped her own destiny.

Jade broke the silence. "Wow, I knew Lord de Winter was astute, but I've never imagined this."

"Yeah, my father's obsession was something else," Alessandra replied. "I wish I knew what to do with all this. Nothing in my training prepared me for this moment. But I know one thing for sure, his disappearance is linked to this. Any ideas, Ash?"

Ash leaned against a nearby bookshelf, his eyes scanning the scattered notes and relics with intrigue and contemplation. "Well, from what I've learned over the years, knowledge is power. And it seems like your father was searching for something powerful. Something that could tip the scales in favour of either light or darkness."

He paused for a moment, his fingers tracing the edges of an ancient talisman. "Perhaps your father's disappearance is connected to the very thing he was searching for. It's possible that he delved too deeply into forbidden realms."

Jade nodded in agreement, her expression thoughtful. "If that's the case, then we must tread carefully. Whatever your father was involved in, it attracted powerful forces. And they won't hesitate to eliminate anyone who poses a threat to their agenda."

Alessandra's eyes sparkled with determination and uncertainty. "I won't let fear paralyse us. My father dedicated his life to protecting the realms, and I will honour his legacy by continuing his work. We have to find out what he was searching for and uncover the truth behind his disappearance."

Ash offered a reassuring smile. "You're right, Alessandra. We may not have all the answers now, but together, we'll navigate this intricate web of mysteries and secrets. We'll follow the clues, consult the notes, and seek any allies who can shed light on your father's path."

Jade stepped forward, placing a hand on Alessandra's shoulder. "We're with you every step of the way. Whatever challenges lie ahead, we'll face them together, as a team. We won't let anything or anyone stand in our way."

Alessandra's firmness solidified, her gaze reflecting a newfound strength. "Thank you both. Your support means everything to me. Together, we'll uncover the truth, protect our world, and bring my father back."

With a smile gracing her lips, Alessandra shifted

her attention back to the desk. Her hand extended, fingers delicately brushing against the weathered leather of the journal's cover. A subtle shiver coursed down her spine, as though the touch itself had summoned her father's spirit, infusing the pages with his soul.

As she lifted the journal from its resting place and cradled it in her hands, she noticed it bore the marks of a well-loved companion. The weight of the journal was reassuring—could it hold the answers she had long sought?

Alessandra carefully opened the notebook, revealing handwritten script adorning the pages. Each pen stroke spoke of her father's meticulous nature, his dedication to documenting thoughts and discoveries. The scent of aged paper mingling with faint ink filled her senses - a heady mix of nostalgia and purpose.

As she turned the pages, her eyes fell upon a particular entry, its title drawing her attention. There, in the elegant cursive script, was the letter she had been searching for—the words penned by her father, preserved within the confines of the journal.

My Dearest Lucien and Alessandra.

If this letter has reached your hands, it signifies that the time has arrived for you to unravel the final pieces of the intricate puzzle I've left in my wake. As your father, it pains me to communicate with you from the realms beyond, yet I must emphasise the gravity of the mission at hand.

Even before embarking on this expedition, I possessed foresight regarding my own destiny. I understood that my path would culminate in an untimely conclusion, but I willingly embraced this sacrifice for the greater good. Now, it is my solemn responsibility to disclose the whereabouts of my resting place, a tomb of profound significance and the crucial key to locating the weapon capable of shifting the tides against the Order.

Beneath the very foundations of our ancestral estate lies a concealed labyrinth of catacombs. A sacred realm untouched by the passage of time. It is within these forgotten depths that my final abode resides. The catacombs house the enigmas of our family's heritage, and within their ancient walls, you shall unveil the clues that shall steer you towards the true might of the weapon.

I implore you, my dear offspring, to exercise caution as you traverse the catacombs. The serpentine corridors and dilapidated passageways teem with perils, while the ethereal beings dwelling within serve as both guardians and gate-keepers of our family's secrets. Show reverence in their presence, and they shall serve as your guiding light towards the heart of the tomb.

Once you reach the inner sanctum, an altar bathed in otherworldly luminescence shall greet your sight. It is there that the ultimate key awaits you—a symbol of our shared purpose and the culmination of my life's labour. Concealed within these sanctified walls lies the weapon you seek. An inexhaustible source of power capable of shattering the Order's dominion over our realm.

Yet, remember, my cherished children, that the weapon is not solely an instrument of annihilation; it represents hope—a beacon that shines even amidst the darkest of hours. Wield it with compassion, and a dedication to justice. Allow our family's legacy to guide your actions, and let love and unity be your guiding principles.

As you embark upon this arduous voyage, know that my ethereal presence shall walk alongside you. Draw strength from our unbreakable bond, from the love coursing through our veins. Allow it to be your shield against the tribulations that lie ahead, for your hearts are pure and your determination resolute.

Lucien, my son, your unwavering loyalty and unyielding grit, shall serve you admirably. Alessandra, my daughter, your resilience and indomitable spirit have forever been a well-

spring of inspiration. Together, you form a formidable force, destined to affect the transformation our world so desperately craves.

Unravel the secrets concealed within the catacombs, embrace the power of the weapon, and allow justice to illuminate your path. Fulfil our family's legacy and reclaim the equilibrium that the Order's malevolence has disrupted.

With eternal love and belief in your strength,
Your father

Her heart quickened as she read the familiar words, the emotions welling up within her, threatening to spill over. It was a bittersweet moment, a convergence of past and present, of memories and longing.

Alessandra marvelled at her father's profound love, his foresight to leave this cherished message. The letter was a shining beacon, illuminating their path forward. A tribute to his faith in their potential to uphold his legacy.

With trembling hands, she clutched the journal to her chest, feeling the weight of her father's presence within its pages. She knew that within those written words lay the key to their future. A path that would lead them closer to the truth, closer to the weapon that could change the course of their world.

In that moment, Alessandra made a silent vow —to honour her father's memory, to unlock the secrets contained within the journal, and to embark on the journey that lay ahead.

As Alessandra tightly clutched her father's worn journal to her chest, an ominous laughter filled the air. The sound, like nails on a chalkboard, sent shivers down her spine, and her heart skipped a beat as she immediately recognised the distinctive cackle. It could only belong to one creature—Azaroth. He wasn't dead after all.

"So you're alive," Alessandra muttered, her voice laced with surprise.

Azaroth grinned mischievously, his eyes gleaming with amusement. "Yes, Alessandra. Death has a way of being quite temporary when it suits my purposes," he replied, his tone dripping with sarcasm.

Ash rolled his eyes, unimpressed. "You're not funny," he interjected, his annoyance palpable.

Jade crossed her arms, a stern expression on her face. "We're not here to entertain you, Azaroth. What do you want?" she demanded, her voice filled with defiance and impatience.

Azaroth's grin widened, his gaze shifting between the three of them. "Oh, but you are, my dear friends. I will let you in on a little secret. You have been captured by the Order, and this is nothing but a dream."

Chapter 6

VLAD'S ARM REMAINED OUTSTRETCHED, THE BED beside him vacant and cold. His eyes fluttered open, greeted by the sight of dishevelled sheets and tangled blankets, reminders of the night he had shared with Alessandra. He reached out, fingers grazing the pillow that still held the faint impression of her head, a bittersweet reminder of their intimacy.

Closing his eyes, Vlad replayed the sound of her voice, the weight of her words settling in his heart. "I'm sorry. I have to find my father. Please understand." He knew someone must have helped her plant that image in his dream, but he admired Alessandra's courage. She possessed a strength, a fierce need to confront her family's secrets head-on. It both captivated and worried him.

Yet, as his mind traversed the labyrinth of possibilities, a knot of anxiety tightened within Vlad's chest. The dangers posed by the Order and their relentless pursuit loomed large in his thoughts. He believed in Alessandra's resilience, her ability to face whatever challenges awaited her, but the uncertainty of their future cast a shadow over his heart.

With a heavy sigh, Vlad rose from the empty bed, a mix of hope and apprehension swirling within him. His trust in Alessandra's capabilities warred with the ever-present fear of the unknown. He vowed to support her from a distance, to be her silent guardian, while steeling himself for the battles yet to be fought.

The Prince, now dressed, made his way to the headmaster's office, a place that had become his own. In his mind, he silently summoned Angelique, who stood dutifully by the door, awaiting his arrival.

"Your Highness," Angelique said, her voice filled with reverence as she bowed her head, then opened the door and gestured for the Prince to enter.

"Would you be so kind as to summon my nephew, Lucien, and inquire about the whereabouts of my father and Miss Nicolay?" Vlad requested with a sense of urgency.

"I apologise, Your Excellency," Angelique replied, her voice tinged with regret. "Only Monsieur de Winter is present at the estate today."

A surge of restrained anger coursed through Vlad's veins as he heard the news. "What has happened to the other two?" he inquired, his voice carrying a mix of concern and frustration.

"It seems they left the estate last night, along with Miss de Winter," Angelique responded, her tone holding a tinge of sorrow.

A heavy silence enveloped the room, the weight of the revelation sinking in.

"And you allowed them to leave?" Vlad's voice thundered, reverberating through the hallways. The maid stood before him, head hung in shame, unable to offer a response.

"My apologies, Angelique," Vlad said, his voice mellowing, realising that the blame did not lie with her. "You could have done nothing to prevent their departure."

Overwhelmed with guilt, Angelique dropped to her knees, tears streaming down her face. She dared to look up at him, her gaze filled with remorse and a plea for forgiveness. "You don't have to apologise, Master," she whispered, her voice laden with regret. "I should have awakened you the moment I realised what was happening, but... you were sleeping so peacefully. I couldn't bear to disturb you."

Vlad's expression softened, and he offered the maid a compassionate smile. "Do not burden yourself with guilt, Angelique. Your intentions were pure, and you acted out of concern for my well-being."

Tears continued to flow down Angelique's cheeks as she looked towards him, her gaze brimming with sorrow. "I am sorry, Your Highness. Please forgive me," she pleaded, her voice trembling.

Vlad's heart softened further, and he extended a forgiving hand. "There is nothing to forgive, Angelique. You have been devoted to me. Now, please fetch Lucien."

With relief and gratitude, Angelique rose from her knees, wiping away her tears. "Thank you, Your

Highness," she muttered before leaving the room to carry out his request, a renewed strength in her steps.

Lucien entered the office shortly after, his expression stoic and filled with a sense of responsibility. Vlad's gaze met his nephew's, and they both knew they were now faced with a dire situation.

"Uncle... you've heard, I suppose," Lucien began, his voice tinged with disappointment and concern.

"Yes," Vlad replied, his voice reflecting a touch of sadness. "Alessa has proven herself to be quite the independent spirit. Enlisting the help of my father and Miss Nicolay, she has embarked on a daring journey. Although I'm relieved she had the foresight not to go alone, I can't help but feel disappointed she left without a word in the dead of night."

Lucien's face grew darker as he spoke. "That's just the beginning of our troubles, Uncle. Lóthurr, the leader of the Shadowcrest clan, has sent word that the Order has captured them. His spies relayed this information a few minutes ago."

A sinking feeling settled in Vlad's heart as he realised the gravity of the situation. How had the Order captured Alessa, despite having a demon prince and a powerful witch by her side? It spoke volumes about the growing strength and cunning of their adversaries.

Vlad's voice trembled with desperation and determination. "We must bring her back, Lucien, no matter the cost. Have the Order made any demands or communicated their intentions?"

Lucien shook his head. His expression hardened. "Not yet. It seems they want to keep us in the dark. But we can't afford to wait. We must act swiftly to rescue Alessa before they carry out whatever sinister plans they have in store."

Vlad's eyes narrowed, his mind racing with thoughts of strategizing and gathering allies. "We will find her, Lucien. I swear it. We will assemble a team, reach out to our contacts, and leave no stone unturned until Alessa is back safely by our side."

With a renewed sense of purpose, Vlad and Lucien locked eyes, their willpower mirrored in their gazes.

"What are you thinking?" Vlad asked, his voice filled with concern and a touch of apprehension.

Lucien paused for a moment, gathering his thoughts before responding with a resolute tone. "I have seen firsthand how the Order can manipulate their knights and turn them against their own. It wouldn't be impossible for them to do the same with Alessandra."

Vlad's brows furrowed, his mind grappling with the gravity of the situation. "Do you believe they would go to such lengths?"

Lucien's gaze hardened, his conviction unwavering. "I believe so. We have amassed a formidable alliance of supernatural beings, and Alessandra has discovered and unlocked her true powers. It appears we may have gained an advantage. Perhaps the Order fears losing control."

A feeling of disquiet came over Vlad as he considered the possibility of the Order resorting to such extreme measures. The thought of the love of his life enduring torture and manipulation sent a chill down his spine.

"Breaking someone through torture is a horrific task," Vlad murmured, his voice laden worry and anger.

Lucien nodded, his expression solemn. "Indeed, it is. I know this personally. When an assassin went rogue in the past, they sent me to apprehend him. I brought him back, but the transformation he underwent in the dungeon was so severe that he became unrecognisable."

Vlad took a deep breath, exhaling slowly as he

tried to steady his racing thoughts. "Thank you, Lucien, for keeping a level head in this tumultuous situation. I know it's difficult, but we must stay strong for Alessandra. I believe she possesses bravery that will sustain her until we bring her back. And as for Avery, something deep within me tells me we will find her soon enough."

They stood wordlessly, the silence heavy with their unified resolution and shared anticipation. Despite the risks and uncertainties that lay ahead, Vlad made a tough decision. He knew that Alessandra's life hung in the balance, and he couldn't bear the thought of her suffering at the hands of the Order any longer. Fortitude burned in his eyes as he turned to Lucien.

"Lucien, I can't stand idly by while your sister remains captive. I will go after her and bring her back, no matter the cost," Vlad declared boldly.

Lucien's brows furrowed, worry etched on his face. "But Uncle, it's far too dangerous to go alone. We need a plan."

Vlad's hand tightened on Lucien's shoulder, gratitude and concern flickering in his eyes. "Lucien, I need you to stay here at the academy while I embark on the journey to rescue Alessandra.

You must remain vigilant, for news of Avery may come at any moment."

Lucien nodded, his expression serious and resolute. "I won't fail you. I'll keep a watchful eye and gather every bit of information that comes our way. We won't let the Order slip through our fingers."

A glint of reliance and tenacity flashed between them—brothers-in-arms conferring without words.

"I have faith in you, Lucien," Vlad avowed, his tone laden with certainty. "You're a capable leader. The academy and our allies will stand strong under your steadfast guard." He gripped Lucien's shoulder, his words steeled. "And together, we will see Alessandra and Avery safely returned. Of this I am sure."

As Vlad observed Lucien's resolute demeanour, a sense of pride swelled within him. The weight of responsibility settled upon his nephew's shoulders, yet Lucien stood tall, ready to face the challenges that lay ahead. Vlad couldn't help but marvel at the transformation he had witnessed in him, from a young and uncertain recruit to a formidable man, and soon to be a leader.

A flicker of worry passed through Vlad's mind as he contemplated the dangers that awaited him on his solitary journey. He couldn't shake the gnawing fear of the unknown, the lurking shadows that threatened to consume him.

Bracing himself for the treacherous road ahead, Vlad fortified his resolve. Thoughts of Alessandra's courage and resilience echoed in his mind, bolstering his determination. He pledged to himself that he would not rest until he had rescued her from the clutches of the Order.

As Vlad turned to leave, he uttered a silent prayer, a plea to the fates to keep Lucien safe and guide him through the trials that awaited. He knew their destinies were intertwined, and that each played a vital role in the grand tapestry of their mission.

Chapter 7

VLAD CONTEMPLATED THE IDEA OF BRINGING HIS loyal knights along on his journey to the Order's current stronghold, Corvin Castle. However, after careful consideration, he dismissed the notion. Travelling with a horde of vampires was a sure way to attract attention, and discretion was of utmost importance in his mission. After all, the element of surprise could be a powerful weapon against their nefarious enemies.

Within the hallowed halls of Roslyn Academy, nestled in a forgotten corner, lay the Sanctum of Sylnor Relics—a chamber steeped in mystery and brimming with the remnants of ages long past. Stepping into the chamber illuminated by flickering torchlight, Vlad's eyes surveyed the meticulously organised shelves, each cradling a relic of untold power and ancient significance. The air crackled with a tangible energy, as if the artefacts themselves held dormant magic.

Amidst the display, Vlad's attention was drawn to an amulet, its craftsmanship unparalleled. Embedded within its intricate design were sigils of protection and wards against supernatural forces. Legends spoke of its origins, tracing back to a long-lost civilization renowned for their mastery of enchantments. As Vlad clasped the amulet around his neck, he felt a subtle hum resonating through his being. The item shrouded him in a shield, making him invisible.

Venturing deeper into the chamber, his gaze settled on a tome resting upon an ornate pedestal. The pages contained cryptic incantations and forbidden knowledge, which ancient scribes had laboriously transcribed. The tome exuded an aura of forbidden power, a tantalising glimpse into the secrets of prohibited magics. Vlad traced his fingers over the text and absorbed the arcane wisdom that ancient scribes had carefully preserved across the ages.

And then, his eyes fell upon the Blade of Mystoria, a weapon of extraordinary craftsmanship and mystical properties. Crafted from a rare alloy infused with magical essence, the sword shimmered with an ethereal radiance. Its edge was honed to perfection, capable of slicing through enchantments with surgical precision. Etched along the blade were sigils of binding, channelling the raw elemental forces into a potent strike against supernatural adversaries.

As Vlad grasped the hilt, power surged up his arm, intertwining with his very essence. The blade seemed to resonate with his presence and was attuned to his command. It was not just a weapon; it was an extension of his will, a conduit for his magical prowess.

Vlad's thoughts were consumed by Alessandra, filled with an inflexible desire to rescue her, regardless of the price he had to pay. The connection they had formed during their treacherous quest had evolved into something profound, a bond that surpassed the dangers they faced.

With his heart ablaze and his mind focused, Vlad embarked on a relentless pursuit to rescue the woman who had captured his soul. The journey would be perilous, but he knew that the power of their connection would carry him through. For Alessandra, he would face any danger, defy any obstacle, and prove that their love was unbreakable.

For three consecutive nights, Vlad embarked on a harrowing odyssey to the forbidding gates of Corvin Castle in Romania. Beneath the ethereal radiance of the moonlit sky, he traversed hazardous terrains, every step a testament to his purpose. The path that stretched before him was riddled with uncertainty, shrouded in an ominous aura that would have deterred lesser souls. Yet Vlad pressed on, unflinchingly forging ahead, undeterred by the perils that awaited.

As the darkness descended, cloaking the world in an inky veil, Vlad tapped into the depths of his vampiric prowess. His supernatural abilities endowed him with preternatural speed and agility, enabling him to navigate the shadows with uncanny swiftness. To mortal eyes, his movements were a mere blur, an ethereal phantom leaping over obstacles and hurtling through the night. The wind whispered tales of his passage, carrying the echo of his determination across the land.

Throughout those long and gruelling nights, Vlad's senses remained heightened, tuned to the faintest tremors of peril lurking in the abyss of darkness. His keen vampire vision pierced through the veil of night, granting him the ability to detect hidden threats and discern the treacherous paths that led to his destination. Beady eyes watched him from the shadows. Unseen creatures prowled the underbrush, their presence betrayed only by the rustling of leaves and the faintest of growls. Vlad remained undeterred, unshaken by the ominous forces that sought to impede his progress.

With each passing night, Vlad's anticipation swelled, his heart pulsating with a fierce intensity that matched the rhythm of his steps. The moon seemed to watch over him with a benevolent gaze, its gentle light lending him a modicum of solace in the face of the arduous journey that lay ahead.

As he ventured deeper into the heartland of Romania, the supernatural forces that governed the region became more pronounced. The occult realm seemed to converge with the mortal plane, blurring the boundaries between the living and the undead.

Ancient curses and spells lay dormant, waiting for unsuspecting souls to awaken them with their presence.

Vlad's vampiric nature drew attention, like a beacon calling out to creatures that hungered for a taste of his immortality. Vicious werewolves prowled through dense forests, their eyes glowing with feral intensity as they tracked his every move. Cunning witches harnessing dark magic laid crafty traps and wove intricate spells to ensnare any who dared to trespass upon their domain.

As he delved further into the Romanian countryside, Vlad encountered more treacherous adversaries. Vengeful spirits, restless from centuries of torment, materialised with ethereal whispers and bone-chilling moans, seeking to bind him to their tragic fate. Ancient vampires, powerful and malevolent, rose from their slumber, their thirst for blood insatiable and their strength unmatched.

The very landscape itself seemed to shift, transforming into a labyrinth of ominous caves and passages. The earth beneath his feet quivered with latent power, concealing ancient tombs and forgotten crypts, each one harbouring its own guardians and secrets. Danger was imminent, and it carried its scent in the charged energy of the air.

Despite the mounting perils that beset him, Vlad's resolve remained steadfast. He navigated through treacherous terrain, his vampiric abilities his only advantage. The shadows became his ally, granting him temporary sanctuary as he evaded the gaze of his adversaries. His heightened senses detected danger from miles away, allowing him to expect and counter the threats that lurked in the darkness.

As the nights blended together, fatigue threatened to cloud his mind, but Vlad pushed through, drawing strength from the thought of Alessandra's presence at the end of his journey. Her memory sustained him, giving him renewed energy and a resolute purpose that propelled him forward.

Finally, on the third night, as the first rays of dawn painted the horizon with hues of gold and pink, Vlad arrived at his destination. He stood before the imposing gates of Corvin Castle, his heart pounding with relief and anticipation. The long and arduous journey had led him there, and he knew the true test awaited within those ancient walls.

The castle stood proudly against the backdrop of the Romanian countryside, a majestic fortress that exuded both grandeur and an air of mystery.

Its towering walls, crafted from ancient stone, reached toward the heavens, casting a formidable shadow upon the land below.

Its architecture bore the marks of centuries past, blending Gothic and Renaissance elements in a harmonious union. Turrets and battlements adorned its perimeter, standing as sentinels of protection and fortitude. Each stone, weathered by the passage of time, whispered tales of a bygone era of knights and noble aspirations.

As Vlad's eyes lingered on the majestic Corvin Castle, a bitter irony filled his thoughts. The Order chose this remarkable fortress as their seat of power, which marred the grandeur and historical significance of the castle. It was a cruel twist of fate that such a symbol of heritage and nobility had fallen into the hands of those who sought to wield darkness and control. The castle's grounds, once graced by the footsteps of noble rulers and brave knights, now echoed with the whispers of the Order's nefarious plans. It was a desecration of the castle's true legacy, a stain on its storied history.

Vlad couldn't help but feel a surge of indignation. The Order's presence within the castle walls tainted the memories of valour and chivalry that once thrived there. The clash between the castle's noble past and the sinister machinations of the Order created a dissonance that echoed through Vlad's soul.

Yet it was precisely because of the Order's stronghold within Corvin Castle that Vlad's resolve burned brighter. He saw it as a challenge, an opportunity to reclaim the castle's genuine spirit and restore its rightful purpose. It was a personal quest to liberate not only Alessandra but also the castle itself from the clutches of darkness.

Vlad knew that within those walls lay the key to unravelling the Order's plans, the knowledge that would aid him in rescuing Alessandra and thwarting their malevolent agenda. It was a daunting task to confront the very heart of the enemy's power, but Vlad was undeterred. He would face the Order head-on, reclaiming Corvin Castle as a bastion of light and justice.

With his determination steeled, Vlad took a step forward, ready to infiltrate the castle's walls and confront the Order's grip on power. Corvin Castle, despite its current tainted state, held the promise of redemption. Vlad promised to resolve the clash between the castle's noble heritage and the Order's sinister presence, ensuring that honour and righteousness prevailed within its hallowed halls once more.

The ancient weathered wooden gates groaned in protest as Vlad approached, as if reluctant to grant him passage. The sound echoed through the surrounding silence, serving as a sombre reminder of the fortress's age and the secrets it held within.

As the gates swung open, the faint scent of damp stone and aged timber wafted towards Vlad, a tangible invitation to step into the realm of mystery and intrigue that lay beyond. The threshold between the outside world and the enigmatic corridors of Corvin Castle beckoned him forward like a portal into a realm untouched by time.

As Vlad stepped through the solemn gates, an overwhelming wave of memories washed over him, transporting him back to the darkest chapter of his human existence. The image of his tattered form, dressed in rags, with a face battered, dirty, and drenched in his own blood, resurfaced in his mind. It was the day when his life had shattered. The day Bran Castle had fallen to his enemies.

On that fateful day, he had found himself on his knees, tears streaming down his face. A desperate plea had escaped his lips, begging for his beloved wife's life to be spared. But the cruel hands of fate had dealt him a devastating shock. The news had come, a crushing blow to his shattered heart, that she had taken her own life. In that moment, something inside Vlad had broken beyond repair.

The memory of a heartless soldier, fuelled by sadistic pleasure, relentlessly delivering kicks upon kicks, flashed before his eyes. He could never forget the pain and humiliation the heartless man had caused him. But it was the crushing weight of learning of his wife's tragic fate that had driven him to the edge of despair.

In the depths of his anguish, Vlad had made a dangerous pact. His own blood, mingling with his tears, had become a macabre offering, a plea to the infernal realm. With a trembling hand, he had summoned Asmodeus, the Dark Prince himself, and laid his own life on the line. He had offered himself as a weapon, a vessel for vengeance, in exchange for the chance to punish his enemies and keep his flickering flame of life burning.

Love, he realised, was a bitter and blind mistress. Despite his wife's cruelty, he had loved her with an intensity that defied reason. The heart could be a foolish moron, blindly grasping at love even in the face of suffering.

The memory of that pivotal moment lingered, a

haunting reminder of the price he had paid, of the darkness that now coursed through his veins. As Vlad stepped further into the depths of Corvin Castle, the weight of his past and the promises he had made bore down upon him. It was time to settle the score, to make his enemies pay for the unspeakable horrors they had unleashed upon him.

Every step he took echoed with purpose, resonating with the weight of his past sufferings. No longer would he be the helpless victim at the mercy of his tormentors. This was the turning point. He would rise from the ashes of his past and unleash a storm of retribution upon those who had shattered his life.

The castle's shadows whispered his name as if beckoning him to embrace the darkness that had consumed him. Vlad, now a creature of the night, wielded a newfound power, honed by the trials he had endured.

As if sensing his presence, the sun-drenched courtyard suddenly came alive with a legion of knights, their polished armour gleaming under the radiant rays. Their swords were drawn, their eyes filled with steel and confusion as they confronted the enigmatic figure before them. Vlad's lips curled into a smirk, his eyes glinting with an eerie intensity.

With a swift motion, Vlad extended his arm, palm facing the sunlit sky, and closed his fist. A surge of dark energy crackled through the air, casting an ominous shadow upon the once-bathed courtyard. In an instant, the knights' legs buckled beneath them, their bodies collapsing to the sun-kissed ground with bone-shattering thuds.

It was a paradoxical sight, the clash of sunlight and darkness, as the fallen knights writhed in pain, their voices echoing with cries of anguish and confusion. Vlad's gaze softened, a flicker of remorse passing through his eyes. They were unwitting victims, entrapped by the false promises and manipulation of the Order they so faithfully served.

Yet, Vlad knew that to rescue Alessandra and exact his long-awaited retribution, he had to confront these obstacles head-on. The bonds of knighthood still held sway over his own heart, but his allegiance to justice burned brighter than the midday sun. He saw himself as a renegade knight, a warrior of truth, standing against the corruption that permeated the very organisation these knights represented.

Drawing upon his own experiences and the depths of his power, Vlad approached the fallen knights with a mixture of caution and compassion.

In that moment, he yearned for these men to awaken from their slumber, to see through the veil of deception that had ensnared them. With unwavering firmness, he whispered words of redemption, hoping that someday they would break free from the chains that bound them and join him in his quest for justice.

As the courtyard fell silent, save for the gentle rustle of the wind through the sunlit leaves, Vlad took a moment to gather his thoughts. The battle had only just begun, and the weight of his mission rested heavily upon his shoulders.

Chapter 8

Consciousness crept back as Alessandra's eyes flickered open, her mind fogged with disorientation. As the blurred forms around her coalesced into sinister clarity, icy dread seized her heart. She was suspended in an iron cage, hanging lifeless in a vast chamber lit by guttering torches. Rusty shackles gnawed her wrists, sending spikes of agony through her rigid body.

Nausea roiled within as recognition dawned—she was a prisoner in this macabre dungeon. A lamb brought to slaughter. Shadows danced around her, warped into leering faces by the erratic firelight. Rusted implements of torture glinted on the walls, awaiting her flesh and screams. The sadistic hunger in this room was palpable, like a predator toying with helpless prey.

The fetid air assaulted her nostrils, thick with the stench of mildew and crumbling stone. The relentless drip of water reverberated through the chamber, each echo a taunting laugh at her predicament. She was alone. Jade and Ash had disappeared without a trace, leaving her to fend for herself in this nightmare prison.

In the darkness, she could hear the skittering of rats, their claws scraping the cold stone floor as they scavenged for food. She shuddered at the thought of their beady black eyes watching her, just waiting for her to drop her guard.

Fear gnawed at her insides, tightening its grip as she strained against the merciless chains holding her captive. The frigid metal links seemed to taunt her futile struggles for freedom. The burden of isolation weighed down upon her, amplifying her vulnerability and helplessness.

A nagging ache of concern took root within her, tinted with a haunting sense of loss. Had they endured the same fate? The uncertainty plagued her thoughts, feeding her escalating disquiet. Their faces flashed in her mind, their absence a hollow void in her spirit.

"Is anyone here?" Alessandra's voice trembled with apprehension. The heavy door groaned open, revealing Vlad's imposing figure. The flickering torches cast dancing shadows on the cold stone walls, heightening the tension in the air.

Vlad's eyes met Alessandra's, a glimmer of regret briefly crossing his face before he lowered the cage and swung open its door. As he encircled her in his arms, Alessandra's heart skipped a beat, feeling a mix of relief and confusion. She was briefly tricked into feeling safe by the warmth of his hug.

The metallic sound of a dagger being unsheathed echoed, signalling an impending threat. The hushed gasp that escaped Alessandra's lips mingled with the tense stillness as if the chamber itself held its breath, bracing for the irreversible shift in their fates. He thrust the blade into her abdomen while looking her in the eye.

"Why?" Alessandra's voice rose above a whisper,

filled with disbelief. Her eyes searched his face, longing for answers that seemed to elude her grasp.

Vlad's grip tightened on the dagger, his voice now laced with a chilling edge. "You've ruined me more than the Order did, and I will make you pay for it," he declared, his words slicing through her heart more than the sharp blade.

It was a moment frozen in time, brimming with a storm of emotions. The lingering echoes of their voices, haunted and tinged with anguish, hung in the air, blending with the suffocating atmosphere of the chamber. Alessandra stared into Vlad's eyes, the truth of his intentions etched upon his face.

She closed her eyes, summoning her inner strength amidst the chaos of the chamber. Her voice, a mere whisper, carried a resolute tone as she spoke. "You're not him. Nice try, Azaroth."

A knowing smile played at the corners of her lips, defying the darkness that surrounded her. In that moment, she pierced through the facade, unravelling the illusion that had been crafted to deceive her with her resilience and spirit.

Azaroth's confident demeanour faltered for a fleeting moment, a flicker of surprise crossing his face. The power of her revelation reverberated through the air, shattering the illusion he had woven around them. Despite his malevolent intentions, Alessandra remained steadfast in her knowledge, refusing to succumb to his deception.

The demon's smile widened, a sinister glimmer in his eyes as he responded to Alessandra's defiance. His voice dripped with dark amusement. "Ah, my dear Alessandra. How delightful it is to witness your tenacity. I wonder, how many times can you endure this torment without losing your precious mind? Let's put that to the test, shall we?"

Alessandra's gaze remained steady, unyielding in the face of his taunting words. She knew the magnitude of the trials that awaited her, the depths of darkness he would unleash upon her. But she refused to let fear consume her.

Days blurred into nights, and Alessandra found herself lost in a perpetual haze of uncertainty. Azaroth's relentless torment had eroded her sense of time, leaving her trapped in a disorienting void. The dungeon walls seemed to close in on her, whispering eerie secrets and echoing with haunting cries.

Unable to distinguish reality from illusion, Alessandra's mind teetered on the precipice of sanity. She paced the confines of her cell, her steps faltering, her fingers trailing along the cold, damp stone. Shadows danced along the walls, their shifting forms mocking her fragile grasp on reality.

A cacophony of voices echoed through the chamber. Whispered taunts and haunting laughter reverberated within her mind. Alessandra clutched her head, trying to drown out the tormenting echoes, but they only grew louder and more insistent. Time had become an elusive spectre, slipping through her fingers like grains of sand.

In her disoriented state, Azaroth took advantage of Alessandra's vulnerability, appearing before her in the guise of Vlad as many times before. His voice, laced with deceit, cut through the suffocating silence. "My dear Alessandra, can you no longer discern truth from fiction? Is your mind unravelling like a fragile tapestry?"

Alessandra's eyes darted around the chamber, searching for a glimmer of reality amidst the swirling chaos. "You won't break me," she whispered, her voice resolute. "I will not surrender to your twisted games."

Azaroth's laughter filled the air, bouncing off the walls and invading her senses. "But I already have. I have ensnared your mind, twisted your perception. There is no escape from the labyrinth of illusions I have spun around you."

Fear clawed at Alessandra's heart, threatening to consume her. She struggled to find a semblance of truth, to cling to the memories that anchored her to her identity. But with each passing moment, the line between reality and illusion blurred, slipping through her grasp like smoke.

She closed her eyes, desperately seeking solace in the depths of her own mind. Slowly, a fragment of clarity emerged. Alessandra mustered her strength and silenced the voices that assailed her.

"I am not alone," she whispered, her voice filled with defiance. "I will find my way back. Your illusions cannot extinguish the fire within me."

Azaroth's facade wavered for an instant, a flicker of frustration crossing his face. He swiftly regained his composed demeanour, his eyes gleaming with wicked delight. "My dear Alessandra, how amusing it is to witness your struggle! But mark my words, the darkness will consume you. I am patient."

As Azaroth dissolved into the ethereal mists, Alessandra clung to the fragment of clarity, vowing to reclaim her sanity and pierce through the veil of deception. Though trapped within the labyrinth of her own mind, she resolved to emerge stronger, defying the darkness that sought to devour her.

Alessandra sank to her knees, overwhelmed by the weight of her torment. The walls of the dungeon seemed to close in around her, their suffocating presence stifling her every breath. Hot tears streamed down her face, mingling with the dirt and grime that coated her skin.

"I can't do this anymore," she choked out, her voice raw with anguish. The relentless onslaught of illusions had worn her down, chipping away at her resilience, and now her spirit crumbled beneath the weight of despair.

Amid her breakdown, the demon materialised once more, his visage a cruel mockery of Vlad's. He circled her like a predator, his eyes gleaming with sadistic pleasure. "Ah, Alessandra, look at you. Broken and defeated. How easily the mighty fall."

Alessandra lifted her gaze, her eyes red and puffy from her tears. "Why? Why do you take such delight in tormenting me? What have I done to deserve this?"

Azaroth's lips curled into a malevolent smile. "Deserve? Oh, it's not about deserving. It is about power. I relish in the power I hold over you. In the control I exert over your very sanity."

She trembled, her voice quivering with a mix of

fear and anger. "You're a monster. A heartless creature who thrives on the suffering of others."

Azaroth laughed, the sound grating on her already frayed nerves. "Yes, my dear, that is precisely what I am. And you, Alessandra, are my prized possession. A delicate toy I can manipulate at my whim."

Alessandra's anguish turned into a burning rage. Through tear-filled eyes, she glared at Azaroth. "I will not allow you to break me. I will find the strength to defy you, no matter the cost."

Azaroth's expression shifted, a flicker of annoyance crossing his face. Yet, he maintained his composed facade, relishing in the emotional turmoil he had wrought. "How amusing it is to watch your futile resistance. But mark my words, Alessandra, your spirit will crumble. There is no escape from the darkness that surrounds you."

With a final mocking smile, Azaroth vanished, leaving Alessandra alone in the desolate dungeon. She remained on the cold, damp floor, her body wracked with sobs. Her spirit was battered but not yet broken. Through the depths of her despair, a tiny ember of hope glimmered, a spark that refused to be extinguished.

Torment and despair consumed Alessandra's

mind as she stood in the chamber, and a profound darkness enveloped her. As if a veil had been lifted, Alessandra felt a side of her that had long been suppressed. The weight of her past traumas, the pain of betrayal, and the relentless manipulation she had endured unleashed a torrent of emotions within her.

The ember of resilience and hope that once burned bright within her now wavered, threatened by the encroaching darkness. She felt a sinister presence whispering in her ear, coaxing her to embrace the shadows, to let go of her inhibitions and surrender to the seductive allure of power.

Alessandra's eyes, once filled with determination and kindness, now gleamed with a haunting emptiness. Her laughter echoed through the chamber, a chilling sound that sent shivers down the spines of even the most hardened souls. Her every movement became erratic, as if she danced to the rhythm of her fractured psyche.

She was no longer her old self. In her place stood a twisted embodiment of her deepest fears and darkest desires. The world around her warped and distorted, mirroring the chaos within her mind. Reality became a splintered tapestry, where nightmares and memories merged into an indistinguishable haze.

With each passing moment, Alessandra sank deeper into the abyss, her grip on sanity slipping away like grains of sand through her fingers. The lines between right and wrong blurred, morality lost its hold, and the desire for vengeance and retribution consumed her every thought. The wounds inflicted by the Order, who recruited her into this awful world, seared through her being, fuelling the flames of her fury.

The pain she endured became the catalyst for her descent into darkness. Betrayal and anguish intertwined, gnawing at her soul and eroding the foundations of her once noble spirit. The torment she suffered at their hands, both physical and emotional, ignited a fierce fire within her, demanding justice and retribution.

As the memory of their cruel acts played on an endless loop in her mind, Alessandra's thoughts became consumed by a singular purpose—bring down the Order and make them pay for their transgressions. The intoxicating allure of vengeance called to her, promising an end to her suffering and a restoration of balance.

Yet, with each step she took down this dark

path, Alessandra felt herself slipping further away from her former self. The tendrils of anger and hatred wrapped around her heart, constricting it with a vengeful grip. The clarity she once possessed wavered, eclipsed by a thirst for revenge that threatened to drown out her reason and compassion.

Amid her internal turmoil, doubts crept in like insidious whispers in the shadows. Was her pursuit of vengeance blinding her to the consequences? Was she losing sight of the very ideals she held dear? The weight of these questions bore down upon her, causing her resolve to waver.

But even in the face of uncertainty, Alessandra remained resolute. The pain inflicted upon her had stoked a fire that could not be extinguished. It burned with a ferocity that fuelled her every thought, urging her forward on this perilous journey.

As she continued to descend into the depths of her own darkness, Alessandra knew that the path she walked was fraught with danger. The wounds inflicted by her enemies were deep and raw, festering with rage and sorrow. But she refused to be defined by their cruelty. Instead, she would wield her pain as a weapon, channelling it into a relentless pursuit of justice and vengeance.

With each passing moment, as she sank deeper into the abyss, Alessandra's transformation became more pronounced. The girl she once was faded, replaced by a force to be reckoned with, driven by a thirst for retribution. The lines between right and wrong continued to blur, but during the chaos, she held fast to her singular purpose—to make them pay.

Chapter 9

As Vlad stood in the courtyard, the world around him seemed to fade away, his focus narrowing. He attuned his senses to the subtle rhythms of the castle, searching for that familiar echo, that steady cadence that belonged to Alessandra's heart.

His eyes closed, shutting out the surrounding distractions. With each beat of his own heart, he reached out with his consciousness, seeking the elusive connection that tethered him to Alessandra's existence.

As the minutes ticked by, Vlad's focus intensified, his concentration unyielding. He could almost taste the anticipation, the yearning to find her and be united once more. The bond between them pulsed with primal energy, an unbreakable thread that transcended the physical realm and bound their spirits together.

And then, amidst the cacophony of sounds, Vlad's ears caught a faint but unmistakable rhythm. The heartbeat was like the gentle and steady flapping of a butterfly's wings. It was Alessandra.

A surge of hope coursed through Vlad's veins, his heart quickening in response. He opened his eyes, a renewed determination shining in their depths. He had found her, not merely with his senses, but with the depths of his very soul.

With each step, Vlad ventured deeper into the heart of the castle, guided by a combination of his own intuition and the faint echoes of his beloved Alessandra's presence. The corridors, dimly lit by flickering torches, seemed to stretch endlessly, an intricate maze of stone and mystery.

As he navigated the winding path, Vlad encountered ornate tapestries adorning the walls, depicting scenes of battles fought and heroes celebrated. The vibrant colours and elaborate details seemed to come alive, whispering stories of valour and sacrifice. It was as if the castle itself sought to inspire and embolden Vlad on his mission.

After what felt like an eternity of twists and turns, Vlad stood before the entrance to the Knight's Hall. The massive doors loomed before him, imposing and adorned with intricate carvings of knights in fierce battle. He could almost hear the echoes of clashing swords and the resounding cheers that once filled this hallowed space.

With a deep breath, Vlad pushed open the doors, revealing the grandeur of the ancient space. The hall stretched out before him, bathed in soft candlelight that flickered upon the polished stone floor. Long tables lined the hall, draped in rich tapestries and adorned with silverware and goblets; remnants of a time when chivalry and honour reigned supreme.

The air was heavy with a sense of anticipation, as if the very walls held their breath in foresight of Vlad's arrival. Rays of sunlight filtered through stained glass windows, casting vibrant hues upon the walls.

Sat at the largest table in the middle of the

room, on a chair that resembled a throne, was Vlad's younger brother, Radu. The sight of Radu sent a surge of conflicting emotions coursing through Vlad's veins. Memories of their shared childhood filled with laughter and camaraderie were in contrast to the bitter resentment that had grown between them over the years.

Radu's countenance held a mix of authority and weariness, his eyes reflecting the weight of his responsibilities as the head of the Order. Dressed in regal attire, he exuded an air of calculated power, his presence commanding the attention of all those in the hall. The siblings locked eyes, their gazes a silent battleground where years of pent-up emotions waged war.

The knights of the Order, loyal to Radu, stood guard around the hall, their armour gleaming in the flickering candlelight. Their presence served as a constant reminder of the division that had driven a wedge between the brothers.

Vlad's footsteps echoed through the hall as he approached the table, his face a mask of determination. He knew that this confrontation with Radu would be a defining moment, one that would either lead to reconciliation or deepen the rift that had torn them apart.

The silence was only disturbed by the far-off crackling of the hearth and the soft murmurs of the knights as they looked back and forth between the siblings, unsure of what was going to happen.

"Welcome." Radu broke the silence, his voice carrying a hint of arrogance.

"Where are Alessandra and her companions?" Vlad countered, his tone laced with annoyance that simmered beneath the surface. The years of tension between them had carved deep furrows of resentment, and Vlad's patience with his younger brother was wearing thin.

Vlad's piercing gaze bore into Radu, his eyes narrowing in frustration and disbelief. He had come to Corvin Castle to rescue Alessandra and free her from the clutches of the Order. And now, faced with Radu's presence and his seemingly nonchalant demeanour, Vlad's irritation threatened to boil over. He clenched his jaw, the subtle tensing of his muscles visible as he fought to maintain composure.

The Prince's grip tightened around the hilt of his weapon, his knuckles turning white. The subtle movement didn't go unnoticed by Radu, who responded with a condescending smile.

"So you're alive." Vlad's voice dripped with surprise and disdain. He could hardly contain his curiosity, although he dared not show it openly. "I dare not ask what devil plucked you from Hell and placed you at the helm of the Order."

Radu's lips curled into a sly smile. His eyes glimmered with a hint of mischief, knowing full well the impact of his actions. "Ah, dear brother, one's survival often hinges on alliances and a touch of cunning," Radu replied, his voice laced with calculated confidence.

Vlad's annoyance deepened at Radu's cryptic response, his frustration fuelling his desire to uncover the truth behind his brother's newfound position of power.

"You've chosen a treacherous path, Radu." Vlad's words carried a weight of disappointment. "To think you would align yourself with those who have caused so much suffering. It is a betrayal beyond measure."

Radu's eyes hardened momentarily, a fleeting crack in his composed facade. "Betrayal is a matter of perspective, brother," he retorted, his voice taking on an icy edge. "I have chosen the side that guarantees power and control, a path you seem to have forsaken."

"I shall not ask again. Where is she? I hope…" Vlad trailed off.

"You hope?" Radu echoed, a note of curiosity lacing his words. "Ah, your hope may prove to be both your salvation and your undoing."

Vlad's patience reached its limits. His emotions churned within him like a tempest ready to break loose. His grip on his weapon tightened once again.

"I will find her, Radu." Vlad's voice resonated with determination. "And if any harm has befallen her, no force in this world or the next will protect you from my wrath."

"No need to threaten me," Radu retorted with a smirk. "You shall have the pleasure of reuniting with your friends." His words held a veiled promise, leaving Vlad to wonder about his brother's true intentions.

Vlad's mind raced. He knew Radu was cunning and unpredictable, capable of weaving intricate schemes and manipulations. The thought of being reunited with his friends stirred a mix of hope and caution within Vlad. Was this a trap, or did Radu have a change of heart?

"What game are you playing?" Vlad's voice carried a sharp edge, betraying his wariness. "You speak in riddles, but I will not dance to your tune."

"You underestimate me." Radu chuckled, his voice dripping with smugness. "But the truth shall be revealed in due time. Prepare yourself for the reunion you so desperately seek. The stage is set, and the game is afoot."

As the brothers locked eyes, the battle of wits and wills intensified.

Radu's eyes gleamed with anticipation as he motioned to one of his knights, a loyal servant who had pledged his allegiance to the Order. The knight, recognising his master's call, approached the table with a sense of duty etched upon his face.

Radu's voice resonated authority and excitement as he addressed the knight, his words dripping with intrigue. "Is it ready?" he inquired, his gaze fixed upon the knight's attentive countenance.

The knight bowed respectfully before his master, his demeanour displaying a blend of loyalty and eagerness. "Yes, my lord," he replied with conviction. "The preparations have been made, as you commanded. The stage is set. We are waiting for your order."

Vlad's gaze narrowed, suspicion still lingering in his eyes as he observed the exchange between Radu and the knight. The air crackled with tension, each passing moment adding another layer of intrigue to the unfolding events.

"Very well," Radu replied, his voice carrying a

hint of satisfaction. "Bring forth our honoured guest and let the grand performance begin. The time for revelations is upon us."

"If you'd like to follow me, my lord." The knight beckoned, his voice laced with respect and a hint of urgency. Vlad's gaze locked with the knight's, a silent understanding passing between them. With a curt nod, Vlad acknowledged the man's command, ready to confront whatever awaited him beyond the confines of the Knight's Hall.

Radu, his eyes gleaming with anticipation and intrigue, rose from his chair. His movements were fluid and confident. He trailed behind Vlad, a calculated distance maintained between them as they made their way toward the threshold of the hall. The cool air outside greeted them, though the sun cast long shadows across the castle courtyard.

As Vlad's gaze swept across the courtyard, his eyes widened in disbelief and fury. Before him stood a grand stage, a macabre spectacle designed to taunt and torment. The centre of attention were two colossal bird cages suspended in mid-air, their iron bars casting long shadows upon the ground below.

Inside the first cage, his heart sank at the sight

of his father. Once a proud prince, his spirit was crushed under the weight of captivity. The flicker of hope that had ignited within Vlad's heart was instantly extinguished, replaced by a seething rage that burned like wildfire.

In the adjacent cage, his eyes locked with Jade's. Her usually vibrant and defiant gaze was now filled with fear and uncertainty.

The cages swayed gently in the breeze, their occupants trapped and vulnerable, subject to the whims of their captor.

Anguish flooded his veins, blending with a volatile mix of fury and resolve. His fists clenched, knuckles blanching as he struggled to rein in the tempest inside. This was a targeted blow to all he cherished, a ruthless gambit devised to crush his soul and probe the depths of his tenacity.

His gaze darted between the cages, capturing his father's weary eyes pleading for salvation, and Jade's blend of desperation and trust, imploring him to rescue them from torment.

"Wait, wait! Before you say anything, let's not forget about the pièce de résistance," Radu exclaimed, a wicked gleam in his eyes.

Alessandra emerged from the depths of the dungeon, her presence transformed. Clad in a tight-fitting leather ensemble that accentuated her lithe form, she exuded an aura of both danger and allure. Her dark hair cascaded in waves down her back, framing her face like a mysterious veil. Her eyes, once filled with innocence, now gleamed with a fierce determination, like smouldering embers ready to ignite.

In her hand, she wielded a large whip, its coiled leather an emblem of the power she held. With each step, the echo of her boots against the cobblestones resonated through the courtyard, a rhythmic beat that echoed her newfound confidence. Her movements were purposeful, every sway of her hips and arch of her back hinting at a hidden strength.

She carried herself with the commanding presence of a ringmaster at a circus, a master of ceremonies in this twisted game. Her whip cracked through the air, creating an electric anticipation, the sound slicing through the silence like a sharp command.

Vlad's muscles tensed as he felt Radu's hand firmly gripping his shoulder, restraining him from rushing to Alessandra's side. With a glimmer of defiance in his eyes, Vlad turned to face his brother, his voice laced with anger and desperation.

"Enough games, Radu! She's suffered enough at your hands. Release them now!"

Radu's grip tightened, his fingers digging into Vlad's flesh. It was a silent warning that resistance would only bring further consequences. A sinister smile curled on his lips, a twisted pleasure derived from the suffering he inflicted upon others. "But brother, the show has only just begun. We can't disappoint our audience, can we?"

Vlad's jaw clenched. His gaze fixed on Alessandra as she commanded the focus of the onlookers. Her whip cracked through the air with a resounding echo. He knew Radu basked in this sadistic performance, revelling in the chaos he had orchestrated. But Vlad couldn't bear to see Alessandra subjected to further torment, her spirit manipulated for the amusement of their twisted brotherhood.

"You can save one. Maybe... Choose wisely before your lover tears them to shreds," Radu uttered.

Vlad's muscles tensed as he turned to face his treacherous brother, his voice laced with anger and desperation. "You expect me to choose? You think I can condemn any of them to such a fate?"

Radu's laughter echoed through the courtyard,

chilling Vlad to the bone. "Choices must be made, sacrifices must be offered. Such is the price of power." His eyes gleamed with malicious delight.

"Then I choose them all," Vlad uttered, his voice filled with a newfound doggedness.

Chapter 10

As Vlad summoned a surge of his power and directed it towards Radu, he predicted the impact of his attack. However, to his surprise, an invisible barrier materialised in front of Radu, intercepting the blast and preventing any harm from reaching him. The barrier shimmered with an otherworldly energy, revealing the intricate web of dark magic that protected Radu.

Azaroth's voice resonated with a chilling undertone as he addressed Vlad, his words laced with a sinister allure. "Ah, Vlad, my dear brother, it seems time has clouded your perception. Allow me to reintroduce myself. I am Azaroth, a being born from darkness, the harbinger of chaos, and the embodiment of your shattered brother, Radu."

Vlad's eyes widened with shock and dread as the truth of Azaroth's identity unfolded before him. The realisation that his twisted adversary was an amalgamation of his own flesh and blood sent a shiver down his spine.

Azaroth's sinister smile widened, his gaze filled with perverse satisfaction. "Yes, dear Vlad, I hold the memories of your betrayal, the abandonment you inflicted upon your kin. You brought me into his existence through your ambition."

Vlad's features contorted with anguish and remorse as he confronted the consequences of his past choices. The weight of guilt pressed upon him, threatening to suffocate his spirit. He had once believed his decisions were justified, but now he faced the embodiment of his forsaken brother, a stark reminder of the pain he had caused.

"It is fitting that we stand here, facing one another in this twisted dance of destiny," Azaroth continued, his voice a venomous hiss. "Our intertwined paths converge at this moment, and the echoes of our shared past reverberate through the present."

Vlad's resolve hardened, his gaze meeting Azaroth's. "I may carry the burden of my mistakes, the consequences of my actions, but I will not let them define me. I will face you, Azaroth, and put an end to this cycle of darkness that ensnares us both."

Azaroth's voice dripped with venomous mockery as he taunted Vlad, his words cutting through the air like icy shards. "Do you remember the Sultan's court? The place where we both suffered, where we were both prisoners of war. Tell me, brother, do you recall who escaped that wretched fate? It was you, Vlad, who left me behind to face the horrors that awaited."

Vlad's heart sank as the weight of his betrayal settled upon him, mingling with guilt and regret. The memories of that fateful day at the Sultan's court flooded his mind, haunting him like spectres from the past. He could still see Radu's pleading eyes, the desperation etched upon his face as Vlad made his escape.

"I thought of nothing but survival," Vlad murmured, his voice heavy with remorse. "I believed that if I could break free, I could save us both. But I was wrong. So very wrong. I never knew the extent of the horrors that awaited you and the torment you had to endure."

Azaroth's laughter cut through the air, a chilling symphony that echoed with cruel satisfaction. "Survival, dear brother, comes at a steep price. The Turks, in their insidious pursuit of power, subjected me to unspeakable experiments. Each one more sadistic than the last, stripping away my humanity until all that remained was a vessel for darkness."

Vlad's eyes glistened with unshed tears, his heart aching with the weight of his brother's suffering. He reached out a hand, trembling with longing and regret. "Radu, forgive me. I never wanted this for you. I never intended to leave you behind."

Azaroth's smirk twisted into a malevolent grin, his eyes gleaming with malice. "Your words of remorse hold no weight, Vlad. The past cannot be undone, and the torment I endured has moulded me into what I am now. I embraced the darkness to survive, to cling to a semblance of existence."

Tears welled up in Vlad's eyes, a mixture of grief and desperation. "I will find a way to free you, Radu. I will undo the sins of our past and bring you back from this abyss."

Azaroth's laughter reverberated, seeming to mock Vlad's hope. "Foolish, naïve brother. Redemption is an elusive dream, and the path to salvation is paved with blood and sacrifice. The darkness that consumes me now is the legacy of our shared pain."

Vlad's heart shattered, burdened by the weight of his brother's suffering and the realisation that their fates were forever intertwined. Determination flared within him, fuelled by a desperate need for redemption. "I will confront your darkness, Azaroth. I will fight for my brother's freedom and reclaim the bond we lost."

The demon's grin widened, his eyes burning with malevolence. "Fight if you must, dear brother." As Azaroth's wicked laughter echoed through the air, a cloud of darkness surged forth, engulfing Vlad in its suffocating grip. The inky blackness swirled around him, obscuring his vision and sapping his strength. The air turned heavy with malevolence, as if the very essence of evil had taken form.

Vlad's heart pounded in his chest, his senses heightened as he braced himself for the battle that lay ahead. With a primal roar, he summoned his inner power, a surge of energy that radiated from his core. His eyes glowed with an intense determination, piercing through the darkness like fiery beacons.

Amid the swirling abyss, Azaroth materialised, his form wreathed in shadows. His eyes glinted with a feral hunger, his lips curled into a sadistic grin. With a swift motion of his hand, tendrils of darkness shot forth, lashing towards Vlad like venomous serpents.

Vlad's reflexes kicked into overdrive as he dodged and weaved, his movements a symphony of agility and precision. His body moved with a dancer's grace, his muscles coiling and releasing as he evaded each assault. But the darkness was relentless, a ferocious adversary that sought to consume him.

Summoning his own powers, Vlad unleashed bolts of searing light from his fingertips, aiming to disperse the encroaching darkness. The beams of radiance sliced through the shadowy tendrils, momentarily pushing back the encroaching abyss. But Azaroth merely laughed, his voice carrying a chilling edge.

"You think your feeble light can overcome the depths of darkness?" the demon taunted, his voice dripping with disdain. "I am the embodiment of shadows, born from the very despair that festers within human souls."

Ignoring the taunts, Vlad clenched his sword, revelling in the surging power that pulsed within him. He closed his eyes, focusing his energy, and channelled it into his blade. As his concentration peaked, the very essence of his weapon transformed.

The single blade multiplied before his eyes, splitting into thousands of shimmering projections that filled the surrounding air. The courtyard became awash with an ethereal sea of deadly projectiles, each one a glimmering testament to Vlad's newfound strength.

With a flick of his hands, Vlad unleashed the onslaught of shimmering blades, propelling them towards Azaroth. The missiles sliced through the oppressive darkness, piercing the veil of shadows that surrounded his enemy.

The sea of projectiles closed in on Azaroth, their relentless assault tearing through the fabric of darkness. They collided with Azaroth's defences, their radiant light clashing with the malevolent shadows that shielded him.

But Azaroth was no ordinary foe. Like a dancer embracing chaos, he gracefully weaved between the glimmering projectiles, his motions fluid and precise.

Yet Vlad's willpower did not waver. He adjusted his strategy, his mind sharp and focused. With a surge of power, he sent forth a concentrated beam of energy, cutting through the remaining darkness and converging upon Azaroth. The beam bore down upon him, searing through the shadows with its fiery brilliance.

The demon, surprised by the intensified assault, staggered momentarily, his facade of invincibility cracking. The beam pierced through his defences, grazing his form and leaving a burning mark upon his flesh. An enraged hiss escaped his lips as he recoiled from the burning pain.

Vlad seized the opportunity, capitalising on Azaroth's momentary vulnerability. He pressed forward, closing the distance between them with resolute purpose. His sword, still pulsating with the remains of his power, found its mark, slashing through the surviving barriers and striking true.

Azaroth's voice resonated with a commanding tone, cutting through the tension. "Alessandra, heed my call and come to my side. Show everyone where your loyalty stands."

Alessandra's eyes glazed over as the spell took

hold, eroding her will. She stepped forward, taking out a dagger from her boot, her voice devoid of emotion. "As you command, Master. I will fulfil my duty."

Vlad's heart sank, a mix of anguish and desperation filling his voice. "Alessandra, please, snap out of it! Fight against his control. Remember our love."

Alessandra's gaze remained fixed on Azaroth, her movements cold and mechanical. "Love is a weakness."

Azaroth grinned wickedly, revelling in the discord he had sown. "Vlad, your pleas fall on deaf ears. Alessandra belongs to me now. Prepare to face her wrath."

Vlad's eyes burned with determination as he readied himself for the inevitable clash. "If I must face her, then I will do so, hoping our love will prevail. Even in darkness, there is light."

The battle began, each strike punctuated by the clash of weapons and the sounds of swirling energy. Alessandra, under Azaroth's influence, attacked with calculated precision, her blows fuelled by his dark power.

Vlad skilfully evaded her attacks, his movements driven by a mix of self-preservation and a desperate desire to break the spell. "Alessandra, please listen to me! Remember the moments we shared, the bond we forged!"

Alessandra's voice remained detached, devoid of emotion. "You talk too much. Stop playing and fight me!"

With every parry and dodge, Vlad sought to reach the depths of Alessandra's heart, hoping to rekindle the spark of their connection. "Alessandra, remember who you truly are. You are not a pawn of darkness. You are a warrior of light, my love."

As the clash between Vlad and Alessandra intensified, a spark of realisation ignited within Vlad's mind. He knew he had to break the hold Azaroth had over her. With a quick calculation, he feigned a momentary stumble, allowing Alessandra to close in on him.

Seizing the opportunity, Vlad swiftly closed the distance between them, his hands reaching out to cradle her face. In that fleeting moment, their eyes locked, and he poured every ounce of his love, every cherished memory, into that gaze. For a split second, her eyes softened, a hint of recognition flickering within them.

As their lips touched in a desperate, bittersweet kiss, time seemed to pause momentarily. Vlad's heart ached with a blend of trust and sorrow, hoping against all odds that this act of love would break through the shadows and bring Alessandra back to him.

But even as their lips met, Alessandra's hand, still under the influence of Azaroth, remained firm. In a cruel twist of fate, she thrust her dagger forward, piercing Vlad's heart.

Pain seared through Vlad's body as the blade found its mark. He gasped in agony. The taste of blood mingled with the ghost of their kiss as he stumbled backward, his gaze locked with Alessandra's.

Tears welled up in his eyes, a mixture of anguish and love. "Alessa..."

A SUDDEN JOLT COURSED THROUGH ALESSANDRA'S being, shattering the hold Azaroth had over her. Panic gripped her heart as the realisation of what she had done washed over her. She stumbled back, her eyes widening in horror at the sight of Vlad's wounded form.

"No..." Alessandra gasped, her voice trembling with disbelief and regret. She clutched her shaking hands to her chest, her body shuddering with the weight of her actions. The darkness that had clouded her mind for far too long dissipated, and the genuine horror of the situation unfolded before her.

Vlad's brows furrowed, his features contorting with pain as he locked eyes with Alessandra. In that moment of intense connection, a tumultuous storm of emotions surged within him. Anguish clouded his gaze, etching lines of sorrow upon his face as if a weight had settled upon his soul. Yet, amidst the agony, a flicker of understanding danced in his eyes, a glimpse of recognition that spoke of the intricate web of experiences they had shared. The unspoken words in their gaze conveyed a depth of emotion and a profound sense of the complex journey that had brought them to this moment.

Tears welled up in Alessandra's eyes as she fell to her knees, her strength draining from her body. "Vlad... I... I'm so sorry," she choked out, her voice tinged with regret. She reached out a trembling hand toward him, but the weight of guilt kept her from closing the distance.

Vlad's voice, strained and filled with both

sorrow and a flicker of forgiveness, reached her ears. "Alessandra, it's not too late," he whispered, his words carrying a faint glimmer of hope. "Fight the darkness that has consumed you. Remember who you are."

Alessandra's heart wavered between despair and the small spark of hope Vlad's words ignited within her. She realised that her true self had been trapped beneath the veil of Azaroth's influence, and the moment of clarity she now experienced was a precious gift.

Alessandra's voice, laced with newfound strength, echoed through the chaos of the battlefield. Her golden eyes blazed with a radiant light, an emblem of the angelic powers that surged within her. With each passing moment, her steadfastness grew, fuelled by the love she held for Vlad and the desire to free him from the clutches of darkness.

With a wave of her hand, a shimmering golden barrier materialised around Vlad, cocooning him in a protective embrace. The barrier sparkled with divine energy, warding off any harm that threatened to reach him. Alessandra's touch upon Vlad's face was gentle, her fingers tracing a path of reassurance.

"Hang in there, Vlad," she whispered, her voice

filled with tenderness and determination. "You're safe now. I won't let anyone harm you."

Turning her gaze towards Azaroth, Alessandra's countenance shifted from fear to resolve. The weight of her past dances with darkness had transformed into a steely desire to break free from his influence once and for all.

"I have danced to your tune for far too long," she declared, her voice ringing out with a strength that belied her previous vulnerability. "But today, the music changes. It's time for you to face the consequences of your actions."

Alessandra unleashed her angelic powers, gathering the pure energy within her being. Golden light radiated from her, casting a brilliant glow upon the battlefield. Wings of light unfurled from her back, their ethereal beauty contrasting with the darkness that had threatened to consume her.

With a swift movement, she lunged at Azaroth, her movements fluid and graceful. Her whip crackled with celestial energy as it whirled through the air, lashing with precision. With every strike, the burden of liberation and justice resonated, showcasing her newfound strength and need to break free from the shackles of control.

The battlefield was a symphony of chaos and

fury, the clash of powers resounding through the air. Alessandra, now fully unleashed in her angelic form, stood tall and resolute, her eyes ablaze with a righteous fire. The weight of her past struggles and the battles fought echoed in her heart, fuelling her determination to bring an end to the darkness that had plagued her.

Azaroth, his once confident demeanour now tinged with uncertainty, met Alessandra's gaze. His dark eyes flickered with a blend of desperation and defiance. "You think you can defeat me, little angel?" he sneered, his voice laced with arrogance. "You're just a mere puppet, a vessel for powers you cannot fully comprehend."

Alessandra's response came swift and unwavering, her voice resonating with a clarity that cut through the chaos. "I may have been your puppet once, but no longer. I am guided by love, by the strength of my heart, and the light within me. And that is a force you can never extinguish."

As their powers clashed, Alessandra could feel the weight of her journey, the sacrifices made, and the resilience that had carried her through. She pushed forward, her heart resolute and her will unyielding. The battle was not only a physical one but a battle for her very soul, a testament to her ability to rise above the darkness that had sought to claim her.

"You cannot defeat me!" Azaroth spat, his voice laced with desperation, as he attempted to rally himself. "I am eternal! Darkness will always prevail!"

Alessandra's voice cut through the chaos, filled with a conviction that resonated with the very fabric of her being. "Darkness may linger, but light endures. Love and hope will always triumph over the darkest of shadows."

With a last surge of energy, Alessandra unleashed a torrent of celestial power, a dazzling display of radiant light that enveloped Azaroth. The darkness recoiled and dissipated, replaced by the brilliance of the light she emanated. Azaroth's form exploded and turned to dust.

As the last echoes of the battle faded, Alessandra stood amidst the aftermath, her chest heaving with the exertion of her fight. She surveyed the battlefield and the defeated demon who lay in a pile of ash before her.

Alessandra's heart swelled with both relief and concern as she released Ash and Jade from their captivity. She ensured their safety before turning her attention back to Vlad, who lay still beneath the protective embrace of her magic barrier.

Approaching him with gentle steps, Alessandra knelt beside Vlad, her hands trembling slightly as she reached out to touch his face. His features, once filled with determination, now wore the weariness of the battle and the weight of their shared ordeal.

"Vlad," she whispered, her voice laced with tenderness and worry. "You're safe now. We're safe."

Alessandra's panic surged through her veins like a torrential wave as she watched Vlad lying still, unresponsive to her words. Fear clutched at her heart, threatening to drown her in a sea of despair.

"No," she pleaded, her voice trembling with desperation. "Vlad, please. Don't leave me." Her voice cracked, betraying her anguish as she gently shook his shoulder, hoping for any sign of life.

Alessandra's heart pounded against her chest, its rhythm matching the frantic beat of her thoughts. The weight of the moment bore down upon her, pressing against her chest with an unbearable force. Each passing second without a response from Vlad felt like an eternity, amplifying her anguish to unimaginable heights.

The courtyard seemed to close in around her,

the air thick with tension and unspoken fears. Her breaths came in shallow gasps, barely providing the oxygen her trembling body demanded.

Tears streamed freely down Alessandra's face, their salty trails marking her cheeks with glistening despair. The ache in her chest intensified, a visceral pain that tore through her being. Her voice, strained and fragile, echoed in the air, pleading for a sign, any sign, that the man she loved still clung to the thread of life.

The weight of his fate, their shared destiny, settled upon her shoulders like an unbearable burden, threatening to crush her spirit.

With every passing moment, her panic transformed into a desperate resolve. She refused to accept defeat, refused to let the darkness claim the one person who had become her beacon of light in a world that had grown increasingly dim. Her trembling hands pressed harder against Vlad's unmoving form, as if willing her own life force into him, urging his dormant spirit to awaken.

Time seemed to warp and distort, its passage becoming indistinguishable as her hope teetered on the precipice of despair. But just as the darkness threatened to engulf her, a flicker of movement, almost imperceptible, stirred within Vlad. It was a faint pulse of life, a whispered promise that rekindled the dying flame within her.

Alessandra's tear-filled eyes widened, hope flooding her features as she watched Vlad's eyelids flutter. The slightest sign of consciousness sparked a renewed surge of determination within her. She clasped his hand tighter, as if anchoring him to the world they shared, refusing to let him slip away.

"Vlad," she whispered, her voice both a plea and a prayer. "Come back to me. Fight, my love. Fight."

As if in response to her impassioned plea, Vlad's eyes slowly opened, revealing a glimpse of the vibrant soul that lived within. The heaviness that had weighed upon Alessandra's heart lifted, replaced by a surge of relief so powerful it brought her to her knees beside him.

A single tear slipped down Vlad's cheek, mirroring the mix of emotions that flooded their shared space. His voice, weak yet resolute, pierced the stillness, echoing with the strength of their unbreakable bond.

"Alessandra," he croaked, his voice a fragile melody in the air. "I'm here."

Overwhelmed by a cascade of emotions, Alessandra's tears mingled with a smile that bloomed upon her lips. She caressed Vlad's face, tracing the contours of his features with trembling fingertips, grateful for the flicker of life that remained within him.

"I thought I lost you," she confessed, her voice a tender whisper. "But you're here. You're with me."

Vlad mustered his strength, his gaze meeting hers with a fierce steel that mirrored her own. His hand found hers, intertwining their fingers, bridging the divide that had threatened to consume them. In that sacred moment, time stood still, allowing them to savour the depth of their love and the triumph over the trials that had tested their very essence.

"Alessa," he whispered, his words infused with a blend of gratitude and determination. "We've endured the darkest of storms, but we've emerged together, stronger than ever. Our love has defied all odds, and it will guide us as we rebuild and reclaim what was lost."

Tears glistened in Alessandra's eyes as she held tightly onto Vlad's hand, her touch a lifeline that transcended the physical realm. Their intertwined fingers became a symbol of unity and unwavering support, proof that their bond could withstand even the harshest tribulations.

. . .

THE END

HEY, LOVELIES! I HOPE YOU HAD AS MUCH FUN reading *The Assassin Heiress* as I did writing it. I would be forever grateful if you could leave a quick review sharing your thoughts. Your reviews mean the world and help spread the word about my books!

And if you're looking for your next reading adventure, be sure to pre-order *The Veiled Huntress,* which continues the journey.

I'm so grateful for your support. Without readers like you, I wouldn't get to do what I love. Let me know if you have any questions! Until next time, happy reading!

WORD FROM THE AUTHOR

Hello, lovelies!

My heart sings with gratitude that you have journeyed with me through the pages of my books. As a writer who spins tales of enchantment and mystery, I am thrilled to offer you a chance to escape reality and enter into the realm of imagination.

As you delve deeper into my books, you will discover a world of infinite possibility, where love, magic, and adventure abound. My stories will transport you to places you've never been before and introduce you to characters that will linger in your heart long after the final page is turned.

My artistry is not complete without your voice.

Your reviews are like the wind that carries my stories to new heights and helps me connect with readers like you who cherish the magic of storytelling.

So, if my books have cast a spell on you, bewitched you with their charm, or enchanted you with their tales, please consider leaving a review. Your words are the lantern that guides me on my journey as a writer and helps others find their way to the mystical world we have created together.

Thank you, my lovelies, for the gift of your time and imagination. Let us continue to weave enchanting stories that inspire and delight.

Corinne M Knight

xoxo

ABOUT CORINNE M. KNIGHT

I was born in the mystical land of Romania, a place where legends come alive and magic runs deep. As a child, I was entranced by the stories of the supernatural creatures that roamed the Carpathian Mountains. It was no surprise that I fell in love with writing paranormal romance novels, infusing them with the enchanting magic of my motherland.

While I currently reside in the bustling city of Cardiff with my beloved husband, my heart yearns for the rugged wilderness of Scotland. It's a place that ignites my imagination and inspires me to create stories that transport readers to far-off lands, where love, passion, and the supernatural intertwine.

As a fervent student of history, I find inspiration in exploring the secrets of the past. My dream is to one day live in a grand castle where I can immerse myself in the rich tapestry of historical tales and draw upon them to create new and captivating stories.

To keep up with my latest literary adventures and my upcoming trip to the Scottish Highlands, join my newsletter. And for a chance to win magical giveaways and be the first to hear about my latest book releases, come hang out with me!

Also by Corinne M. Knight

Of Knights and Monsters series – Paranormal and Urban Fantasy Romance:

The Dark Heir

The King of the Undead

The Demon Prince

The Assassin Heiress

The Veiled Huntress

More news regarding the series and the world of the Order of the Dragon will be announced soon. Subscribe to Corinne's newsletter to be the first to know.

Milton Keynes UK
Ingram Content Group UK Ltd.
UKHW040857181023
430840UK00001B/19

9 781914 969096